LOVING HART

A BWWM ROMANCE

Standalone

by

THERESA HODGE

Newsletter Signup!

http://amazon.us9.list-manage.com/subscribe?u=ffde15be91b185d57d934a65c&id=1f6b614090

LOVING HART BY THERESA HODGE

Love has chaseth me to the yard of loneliness. I'm here not by choice but because I'm left with a broken heart. Like a bird, I take flight into the night. My whole world is empty and dark. I am just a loner in the night. Unrest found its existence upon my bed of despair. These drops of tears runneth like rain...flowing forlornly into the troubled sea of pain. One day of folly and betrayal leadth my heart astray but not to delight in the day of a heartfelt promise. Flawless beauty turneth to ugliness leaving me blind with a reminisce of how it used to be. Now, my days and nights are dimmed forever, unless a knight riding into the night, will come to rescue me from this pasture of loneliness, wearing a shining full plated armor, jousting away the pain. Who dare loveth me and only me? Who dare conquereth my heart to the end of times? Who dare chaseth my hurt away? Until it's no more...no more...no more...

PROLOGUE

WHITNEY

I toss restlessly upon the canopied bed. My windows are open to let in the midnight breeze, but somehow my brown skin still feels feverish from the heat that permeates the room. "Damn! When is my landlord getting this damn air conditioner fixed?"

I'm beyond angry as I fluff my pillow. Reaching for the pillow, I turn it to bring the cooler side against my cheek. "My rent is too damn high to be living in these conditions," I mutter with disgruntlement. "It's no use. I can't sleep."

I sigh with frustration as I become stickier with the sheen of sweat that glosses over my body. I sit up and place the pillow in my lap as deep-rooted memories assail my brain.

Tony's words from our last date come back to me full force. The words he spoke should've set off a wary feeling within me, but stupidly, I twisted them to mean what I wanted them to.

"Whitney, do you think a man or a woman can be in love with two individuals at the same time?" he'd asked me as we sat across from each other at a restaurant eating dinner.

"No, not really. I do think a person can be in like or lust with someone, even if they love someone else," I answered, looking across the dinner table at him. His sexy kissable lips and neatly shaved facial hair complemented his chiseled face and deep, dark brown eyes. Oh, how I loved looking into his brown eyes.

Tony wasn't a male model but he should have been. He had close cropped, wavy hair that he kept well-groomed at all times. His body was toned and his muscles had a rippling quality, a sign of how he loved to exercise and stay in shape. His skin was free of blemish and he had a sexy goatee that neatly accentuated the bottom of his chin. Yeah, Tony was sexy and one handsome man and I was happy that he was mine.

His straight nose complemented his prominent cheekbones and square chin. Handsome in an understated way, his wide jawline and athletic shoulders spoke of strength. He possessed an unconcealed, grand power and always walked with ambition and authority.

People always remarked that his best feature was his entrancing, warm brown eyes. Tony's deep-set eyes could shine as bright as the night's moon when they filled with desire. At other times, they favored two muddy liquor-filled tumblers of fiery brandy when he was angry. I was happy that I always stayed on the other side of that anger. I guess that's why his company granted him such an important position. He was a great figure of authority that led his team to many successes. He was also quick to make me smile on many of occasions. My musings always got the best of me when I was in the presence of him. But this night, when I looked into his eyes, something else lurked behind his orbs. Something that frightened me. I shrugged it off as me being in my feelings. It was my time of the month, hormones and all, you know.

"Why do you ask, Tony?" I asked as I sipped from my glass.

"Oh, no special reason," he suddenly looked down at the half-eaten meal on his plate, braised lamb accompanied by a mixture of sautéed vegetables.

"Are you sure?" I questioned him.

"I'm sure," he said, but still didn't make eye contact with me.

"I've been looking at travel brochures for our trip to Aruba next Summer. There are all sorts of exciting things we can do," I said with excitement entering my voice.

"About that," he started to say but I cut him off, my excitement pouring in.

"We can even book our flight now and make our hotel reservations. If we make the arrangements this early, we get a thirty percent discount on the airline of our choosing and a twenty-five percent discount on our hotel fee. Isn't that great, honey?"

"Just peachy," he replied and shoved a piece of steamed broccoli into his mouth. "I forgot to tell you that I'll be away on TriTek business for two whole weeks."

"Aw, really? What do they have you working on?" I asked, pouting.

"It's a special project that I can't discuss at this point," Tony said.

"I'm going to miss you. If I didn't have such an important project coming up with Happy Faces Happy Hearts Daycare, I'd come with you. But as it stands, the project will take Sierra and I at least a month to complete."

"I wouldn't dare want to take you away from making that money," he replied, just before his cell phone chirped, cutting off further conversation. He removed the cell from his clip at his waist and quickly stood up. "I really need to take this call; I'll be right back."

Fifteen minutes later, Tony finally waltzed back to our table. "Dang, it took you a long time."

"Yeah, something's cropped up at the office that I really need to take care of," he muttered as he signaled for the waiter to take care of our bill. "Ready?" he asked. "I'll drop you off at your apartment.

"O-kay," I said slowly. "But I thought we were going to spend the rest of the night together."

"I would love to, but you know how it is when work calls."

"You can still drop me off at your place, can't you?"

"That won't be a good idea. I'll probably be pulling an all-nighter," he replied.

"Too bad," I sighed.

He drove me home in relatively silence. He didn't even walk me to the door or give me a good night kiss. I wondered, how the hell I didn't pick up on his odd behavior and the amount of voice messages I left him on his cell that he never returned. He always contributed it to being busy at the office each and every time. To think back to that night, Tony seemed relieved when I told him about my project and he seemed in a hurry to get rid of me then and on many other occasions, if I were to really think about it. Hindsight is definitely twenty-twenty...Damn, damn, DAMN.

Sighing, with disgust and self-pity, I look over at the clock as I try to clear my mind of my awful thoughts. I notice it's only a little past midnight. It's too late to go for a swim alone, to help take my mind off of what I can't change.

My mother always tells me, "*Whitney, there is a lesson in everything that happens...good or bad.*" With her words echoing in my thoughts, I decide to get out of bed, since I can't sleep anyway. Flipping on the hallway light, I steer my way towards the kitchen on bare feet. I reach overhead into the cabinet to grab me a glass before moseying over to the refrigerator freezer. I grab me a couple of ice cubes to go into my glass and fill it with some tangy Florida orange juice from the fridge. The glass presses to my cracked, dry lips and I take a fortifying swallow. The tangy, sweet juice tastes good going down my throat. I take the glass to press against my cheek. The coolness of the glass feels deliciously calm against my hot flesh.

I walk over to my kitchen window and look out at the moon-filled night. The stars gleam in the sky brightly. Accessing the beautiful night, I note it all. The windless night causes the green leaves on the big oak tree to be still as statues. The waves from the lake in the distance cause the still water to glint like shimmering tiny diamonds. If I was brave enough, I would go for a skinny dip under the midnight moon.

The blaze of heat going up my spine is almost stifling. I set my glass down to remove the thin tank top I have on, along with my panties. I throw them onto the back of a barstool and turn on the tap to rinse my heated face with the cold water in the sink behind the bar area.

A night like tonight makes me desire something, but I don't know quite what it is. I have a good career and I make decent money, even though most of it is tied up in my business with my best friend. It still seems like something is missing. My heart isn't quite whole. It feels like a piece of a puzzle is missing. When I find the missing piece, I'll know what it is I'm missing. Even though I thought I loved Tony, I now realize that I'm better off without him. If he really loved me as he promised he did, he would have never broken my heart. He would have protected it as if it were his own.

My emotions sway inside. There is an urge to let life be…whatever it's going to be. I can't be bitter or give up on love. Maybe, just maybe, my soulmate is waiting to find me. At least I hope he is…

I shake my head of these fantastical thoughts and turn back towards my bedroom. I have to get some sleep if I'm going to be fit to start my day tomorrow. Maybe tomorrow these thoughts of incompleteness will have fled.

Chapter 1

HART

I watch Whitney Martin from a distance. I stand behind a seven-foot-tall, potted plant as its green leaves shield me from view, but I have a clear-cut vision of her as she walks right pass me with another woman by her side. I can't hear what she's saying, but, from her body language and hand gestures, she seems to be in deep conversation with the woman as a frown mars her stunning face.

Whitney was cute as a teenager but she has grown into a gorgeous woman. I wonder, will she remember me if I were to reveal myself to her? My heart pounds with swift acceleration, just like it did years ago when I was a pimpled-face, gawky adolescent. Her dark black, shoulder-length hair frames her face with what seems to be natural curls. They look soft and bouncy to the touch. I wonder what it would feel like to reach out and touch just one. I'm sure that will be a bad idea, so I tamp down my urges.

Her dark-brown skin is glowing with luminosity and health. There's a vibrant, lively, and adoringly irresistible aura around her. It would be hard to miss her; I noticed Whitney immediately when she walked into the building tonight.

I revel in her appearance and how her dress is fitted and clings to every curve of her body. She has on a vivid blue dress that is medium in length with a poufy skirt, empire waistline and short, cropped sleeves. She looks like a beautiful goddess, standing there among mere humans.

Lately, I have been feeling edgy and unhappy energy coursing through me from day to day. I feel inadequate, like something has been missing from my life. My accomplishments in life no longer give me the satisfaction that comes along with me making millions from my business as owner of Hart's Premium Construction Company. My inheritance from my grandfather helped me build my own business from the ground up but my head for business is what helped me quadruple my wealth and run a successful business.

Standing here spying on Whitney, I suddenly feel like a peeping Tom. I can't stand behind this plant all night and track her like I'm some type of predator. It's humiliating enough to think that someone might actually see me spying on a woman I've got a crush on. I ease as unsuspiciously as possible from behind my camouflage and walk right past her.

"I should go get a drink," I mumble when our eyes meet. There's no recognition in her eyes, so I keep on walking. My heart plummets, because I sense she doesn't even remember me. The sudden awareness of her not noticing me is a soundless emotion that sinks inside. How can she not remember me? I spent the majority of my high school years pining away for her. I wasn't a jock back then or very popular with the girls. I may have been a nerd of sorts back then, one who kept to myself quite a bit.

I was nixed from playing sports, because I used to have asthma and had to depend on an inhaler to breathe. But, I've done pretty well for myself. Time definitely has a way of changing things. I'm no longer the shy, pimply-faced teenager, nor do I depend on an inhaler to breathe. I overcame my inadequacies in life. The only thing I never overcame was my love for Whitney Martin.

"Yeah, I should definitely get that drink," I say heading straight to the bar.

Chapter 2

WHITNEY

"OMG, Whit, check out the man over by the terrace doors that keeps watching you."

"Which one?"

"The tall one. He's about six foot three, with the dark black, perfectly groomed head of hair and neat facial hair," Sierra says.

I look over in the direction that my friend is pointing, across the high ceiling room. The man she's talking about is standing in a group of three men chatting. They seem to be in a deep discussion, one raising his hand, the other two very attentive to what he is saying. I wonder what they're discussing to have them as animated as they are.

I take extra notice of the taller, muscular one in the group. His dinner jacket fits him to perfection and his eyes meet mine at the exact time I'm checking him out. He looks like a much younger version of Brad Pitt. He seems molded from a different cast than the other men he's standing with. His skin looks as if it's been intimately kissed by the sun. My eyes are spellbound as I take in this good-looking stranger.

I hurriedly look away and Sierra elbows me in my waist. "Do you know him? He is so Fine, with a capital F," she says, wiggling her brows comically.

"I don't think I know him," I reply as I chance another glance over my shoulder at him. I take notice that he's still staring at me. A tremble courses down my spine from the intense look in his greenish-grey eyes.

"Oh shit, he's coming over," Sierra exclaims, her nails digging into my forearm.

"My arm please! That really hurts, and stop being so loud." I suddenly turn my head back around from the stranger to face Sierra. "Do I have anything in my teeth?" I grin wide so she can inspect my teeth right quick. I don't want any of the spinach I ate earlier to be stuck between my teeth, while I'm greeting this hunk of a man. That'll be too embarrassing.

"No, you're good," she replies quickly.

"Whitney Martin?" The deep gravelly voice says my name as smooth as brandy. Heat curls down my spine with every syllable.

"Do you know me?" I twirl around on my stilettos and crane my neck upward to settle on his handsome face, since my head only stops at his chest. I use this time to inspect the fine, silky hairs on his muscular chest that can be seen from his open-neck striped burgundy and white dress shirt, as he sports a turned down eyelet collar. I notice by his tan that he must spend a lot of time in the sun. His teeth flash white when he gives me a smile.

"You don't remember me at all, do you?"

He looks down at me with disappointment in his eyes and his shoulders visibly slump. A stray lock of his black hair falls over the arch of his thick eyebrow. I feel the instant need to reach out and brush it aside. His hair at the neckline of his shirt has the tendency to curl slightly, I notice this in one full sweep as I check him out. I don't know where the certain urge to run my fingers through his luxurious, silky-looking strands comes from, but I ball my hands into fists to keep myself from doing so.

"I'm sorry, no, I honestly don't. I don't remember you at all," I reply with regret in my voice. I really don't understand how I could forget someone like him.

"Damn, my heart is truly broken," he replies bringing his left hand across his chest. He has a teasing glint in his eyes and a sexy smirk on his lips. I notice his bottom lip is slightly thicker than his top lip, which makes them sexy and kissable.

"I will remember you if you want me too," Sierra says with a giggle.

I look over at her and give her a warning look. The look in my eyes tell her to back off...this one is mine.

The man's smile grows wider from Sierra's words. "I'm Hart Strong." He stretches out his hand towards me with his introduction. I place my hand in his and note he's not wearing a wedding band. "You and I went to Fulton Magna High School together. I was the geeky nerd with the asthma condition that the other kids made fun of. I sat behind you in Mrs. Jones third period English class."

"Hart Strong? Of course, I remember you now! Oh my God, you have changed. I would've never recognized you, if you hadn't reintroduced yourself. It's great to see you again," I say, suddenly feeling a warm and fuzzy feeling inside.

"I'm Sierra Washington, Whitney's best friend," Sierra cuts in.

Looking into Hart's charismatic eyes, I forget my friend is standing by my side. I also realize that Hart is still holding on to my hand, just as he releases it to take Sierra's hand in his.

"Nice to meet you, Sierra." He gives her hand a firm shake before releasing it.

"So, what are you doing these days, Hart?" I ask in an effort to bring his attention back on me.

"I'm into construction. I own and operate Hart's Premier Construction Company. I'm at this mixer trying to win the bid to build the new Children's wing the hospital is having built."

"That's what Sierra and I are here for. We own W & S Interior Decorating & Design business and we put in a bid to do interior design for the Children's wing once it's built," I say.

"Good luck to the both of you. I hope you get it," he replies.

"I hope you get the bid for your company," I say with a smile.

"I hope you get it too," Sierra offers.

"Thank you both. It's been great talking to you two. Maybe you and I can get together for coffee or something," he says while extracting a black business card embossed in gold lettering from the inside of his jacket pocket and handing it over to me. "Both my business and personal cell numbers are on the card. Call me, when you have some free time and we can catch up."

"I'd like that," I reply reaching for the card and slipping it into the small clutch I hold in my hand. "Wow, I can't believe we ran into each other after all this time," I add, while glancing at him again.

"The pleasure has been all mine. Good to see you again, Whitney." The warm look in Hart's eyes as he gives my whole body a lingering glance sets my body to sizzling with heated desire. "Take care, the both of you," he says including Sierra in his glance.

"It's good to see you again too, and take care," I reply before he gives me a sexy grin and walks off to rejoin a group of men he was talking to earlier. I notice the walk, the confidence in his stride and out of nowhere hope flutters and comes alive somewhere deep inside my being.

"Take care," Sierra calls after him and then looks at me. "Well, damn Whit. How in the hell could you not remember a fine ass white guy like Hart Strong?" she asks once he's out of earshot.

"Trust me, if you would have known him in high school, you wouldn't have remembered him either," I reply shaking my head in amazement. The last time I'd seen him, he was a skinny, little guy with red pimples all over his face.

"You may not have remembered him then, but there is no way you will forget his certified banging ass now," says Sierra.

"I know, but I'm going to need you to back down," I warn.

"I'll try, Whit. That man is fione," she mutters, gazing over to where he's standing.

"You are right about that my friend," I agree with her and grab a glass of champagne from a passing waiter off the tray. I tilt the bubbly golden liquid to my lips and finish it in two gulps. God knows I need it to cool off after being in such a magnetic presence such as Hart Strong.

Chapter 3

HART

"Mr. Strong, Mr. Cooper is on line one," Kristy, my secretary alerts me as I stroll into Hart's Premier Construction Company.

"Take a message for me please. I will get back with him as soon as possible."

"Yes sir," Kristy says in a friendly voice, as I enter my office and close the door behind me.

Ever since the night of the mixer for the children's hospital, I haven't been able to get Whitney Martin off my mind. Before the mixer, I'd been over ten years since I saw her last. She looks more beautiful than she did even then. Her radiant brown skin glows with vitality. In fact, had to fight the urge to reach out and stroke the softness of her skin as I stood there talking to her. "Why the hell didn't I ask for her telephone number when I had the chance?" I chastise myself, as I peer around my cozy office. Not getting Whit's number could lead to me spending another ten years without the benefit of touching her, or maybe even infinitely. I'm sure I can track her down, but opportunities like that one is rare.

"Hey, what's up? I saw you come in and had a break. I decided to come in here and check on you. Glad I came in when I did, since you're talking to yourself and all," there is a teasing glint in his eyes when Leo says this. Leo Ferguson walks into my office without knocking like he always does. Leo is also the second boss in command and he's a true commodity with the company.

"If you were to ever knock on my office door instead of barging in, then maybe you wouldn't catch me talking to myself," I reply.

"Whatever." He takes a seat across from my desk without paying any attention to my words. "I just want you to know that I went over everything with the new young employee's that you hired for the summer internship program about what type of equipment to wear for protection when around corrosive and flammable materials. They seem eager to learn and paid close attention to my warnings. I think they're a great bunch this year."

"That's great, Leo. I'm glad to have the kids on board. I think we're in a position to make an impact on their lives. I'm glad we decided to sign up for the cause."

"Yeah, I agree. But whose telephone number should you have gotten?" he asks with curiosity.

"Ah, no one in particular," I say, floundering with my reply. I feel a flush of heat rush up my neckline.

"It sure didn't sound like nothing to me. How is Sabrina doing by the way?" He suddenly changes the subject while staring me hard in the face.

"She's fine the last time I talked to her," I say looking away and picking up a stack of papers that look like they need shuffling to return some semblance of order to them, all of a sudden. There's a slight pause in our conversation. I quickly note that the reports are very well detailed.

"How long have you and Miss High Society been dating each other now?"

"I don't know." I shrug my shoulders. It's not that I don't know how long, it's that the time I've spent with

Sabrina seems to have been all for nothing. "Maybe for about eight months or so now. Why?"

"I just asked," Leo says with a big grin plastered on his face. "I couldn't believe when you said you were dating Sabrina Woods. I didn't think you liked the kind of women who were born and bred with a silver spoon in their mouths."

"Sabrina is okay, most times. She can't help if her family owns half of the Woods department stores across the country," I say, feeling obligated to defend her.

Leo chuckles aloud. "I'm glad I'm not dating someone like her. She'd spend me penniless in a year."

"Don't you have a job to do?" I sit up, giving him a pointed look.

"Yeah, I do boss man." Leo stands up, his fingers resting on the top of the chair. "Catch you later," he says walking out and closing the door behind him.

I lay the papers aside that I'd been shuffling in my hands unnecessarily. I pick up the phone and spoke. "Kristy, you can put me through to Mr. Cooper now."

“Yes, sir,” Kristy replies promptly. “One moment please and I’ll put you right through.”

“Thanks,” I say as I turn my mind towards the business at hand.

Chapter 4

HART

"Darling, how does this swimsuit look on me?" Sabrina spins around in a circle for me to see the fit of the teal blue swimsuit that adorns her body.

"It looks very nice, Sabrina. How much longer are you going to be trying on swimsuits?" I ask her.

"I just want to look my best for your colleague's yacht party, honey."

"The party isn't until next weekend. I thought we were going to get lunch, before going back to my house."

"I know it's not until next week. I might decide not to wear what I get today and then I will have plenty enough time to shop for another outfit next week." She looks at me with her wide blue eyes and flutters her long, mascara-coated lashes at me. *Women.*

"Well, I guess I can see the logic in that," I reply dryly and glance down at my watch. "How much longer are you going to be?" My stomach rumbles loudly as it demands to get fed. I've only had a protein shake and that was before my morning jog as the sun barely rose this morning. But nothing since.

"Okay, I'll have pity on you." She laughs lightly. Her laugh has more of a shrilling, tinkling sound that tends to grate my nerves at times. "Let's go to lunch."

She doesn't have to ask me twice. I jump up from my seat to gather the mounds of clothes she wants to purchase and pull out my black card to decrease our waiting time.

"Will this be all for you today?" The sales clerk sends me a flirtatious smile and I'm brushed to the side.

"That will be all," Sabrina says in a not so nice tone before I can answer. Then she turns to me, perking her lips gracefully. "Thank you darling for my shopping spree."

"You're welcome," I reply and gather her shopping bags to lead us out the overpriced store.

"Welcome to Rathburn's," the hostess greets us once inside the restaurant. "Will there be just the two of you today?"

"Yes," I reply.

"Follow me please," she says before she grabs two menus and leads us to a table. I do a double take as I pass one of the tables. Something leaps inside me. Whitney Martin is sitting at a table having lunch with a woman who seems to be an older version of herself. It must be her mother, I surmise. Our eyes meet briefly and hers widens in surprise once she notices me.

"Hart," the hostess asks us, "is this table suitable?"

Sabrina touches my shoulder to garner my attention.

"Yes...yes, this is fine," I stutter out, finding it hard to take my eyes off the refreshing sight of Whitney. "Thank you," I turn to the hostess before pulling out a chair for Sabrina. I make sure I take the seat facing Whitney so I can keep her in my sights.

"Are you ready to place your orders?"

"Yes," I reply, already knowing what I want before even looking at the menu. "I'll have the parmesan chicken and your house salad."

"What to drink?"

"Ice tea with sugar and one slice of lemon."

"What can I get for you, ma'am?" the hostess asks warmly, turning to Sabrina.

"I'll just have a small salad with a drizzle of fat free dressing, please. Oh, and a seltzer water to drink," she adds.

I frown at her. "Is that all you're having?"

"You know, I have to watch my weight if I'm going to stay looking great in my bikini," she reasons but I continue to frown at her silliness.

"A steak or more sometimes won't harm you, Sabrina."

"I know what I'm doing, Hart," she replies as the hostess takes our menus and promises to be back with our meals soon.

I dig in with gusto, when the food arrives, while Sabrina picks at her small salad like a bird. With only a shred of romaine on her fork, she places it into her mouth and chews. I really don't know how she does it.

My eyes glance up just in time to see Whitney get up from her table. Gathering her handbag, she avoids all eye contact. She perks her lips and steps away from the table. She's walking this way but as she passes our table she keeps looking straight ahead. I frown, because I know she saw me. Why didn't she stop and speak? I sniff the air as a hint of her flowery perfume tickles my nostrils.

"Excuse me." I wipe my mouth and stand up from the table. "I'll be right back. I need to use the men's room," I lie, only because, for some odd reason, I feel urgency inside of me to talk with Whitney.

"Okay, darling," Sabrina replies and immediately goes back to nibbling on her salad like a damn rabbit.

Man, she's leaving, I think as I follow Whitney to the door. By the time I reach it, she's already stepping down from the curb. I stand at the front door with my fingers on the glass and watch as Whitney and her mom slide into their cars and leave the restaurant. A part of me leaves with her.

I walk back to the table feeling bad as I half listened to Sabrina going on and on about some party she wants us to go to tonight. I wish it was Whitney sitting across from me instead of Sabrina. I wonder what she would be saying at this very moment. I imagine the depths of her mind and the metaphoric beauty that comes along with it. I just want to smell her again and look into her eyes.

"Are you finished eating?" I finally ask Sabrina, ready to end the torture of listening to her socialite fantasies.

"Yes, I couldn't eat another bite," she says. I signal the hostess over so I can take care of the bill and tip.

"Let's go," I say to a smiling Sabrina, while thoughts of Whitney are at the forefront of my mind.

Chapter 5

WHITNEY

I checked my appearance in the full-length mirror one last time before grabbing my purse and keys on my way out the door. Today is Saturday and I promised to meet my mother, Rosetta Martin, for lunch at one of her favorite places to eat, which is this upscale restaurant's off Decatur Street called Rathburn's. I felt the need to treat my mother every chance I got.

Since losing my father over a year ago, nothing has been the same for my mother. She works long hours as a registered nurse at Atlanta University Hospital during the week, which leaves her with little or no time to enjoy the leisureliness of life. That's why, most weekends, I try to visit her, no matter how busy I am trying to grow my business.

Before merging into the traffic from my apartment building, I shoot mother a text to let her know I'm just leaving home since she lives closer to the restaurant than I do. I merge onto Interstate 285 into the busy eight-lane traffic.

I cut up my Heart Country and Soul Sirius XM radio station, to listen to the sweet voice of Nashville Star's newest country singer, Sunday Gallenger. Her voice croons out one of her number one hit songs, titled "Reflections." I find myself singing the words with her. *Reflections of what I did right or what I did wrong, tired to pieces of the same ol' song. Yet I listen to it on replay...Over and over, then rewind consistently...*

"You better sing that girl," I say bobbing my head to the only black country singer that sings with deep soul in every song she makes. I smile when I think about how she and the famous country singer Travis Lee got together. It was all over the news and, I have to admit, that's when I fell head over heels with country music for the first time. I guess I can thank Sunday Soul Gallenger for that.

I pull up to the restaurant just as the song ends. When I get out the car, I see my mother parked about four cars over, waving to get my attention. We enter the restaurant and the hostess doesn't waste any time seating us, and taking our orders. It's not long before our food arrives at the table, steaming hot and looking wonderful.

"This lasagna is delicious," my mother says as she forks the delicious food into her mouth.

"I bet it is," I say with a smile as I scan the restaurant. My eyes follow a couple that has just entered and track them to the table directly in front of me. I sigh inwardly as I sense a familiarity of the man in front of me.

Oh, my God, it is Hart! I watch how he takes great care to seat the tall, gorgeous woman that he's with. In that moment, I really wish it could be me. All hope of that happening deflates like a balloon when I realize he has a significant other in his life. *Of course he does,* I berate myself. What successful, good looking man like him wouldn't have anyone in their life? Any woman would be crazy not to snatch him up.

"Earth to Whitney," my mother says, waving her hand in front of my face.

"I'm sorry, mother. Did you say something?"

"I asked you what has the sad look on your face, all of a sudden?"

"Nothing," I answer quickly and force myself to smile. I shake my head to clear the confusing thoughts about Hart. He's someone I hadn't thought about in years…not at all, if I'm being honest with myself. Not until the night of the mixer that is. "How is work going?" I quickly change the topic.

"It's busy…very busy," my mother says. "But my job is fulfilling and I can't ever see myself being anything else except a nurse."

"I'm glad you're happy. You know how much I worry about you."

"I know you do baby and I don't want you to worry about me. I'm truly fine. I'm not going to lie to you; some days get hard, but that's life. It's full of ups and downs, but that only makes me stronger," she says and reaches over to squeeze my hand.

"I love you so much," I squeeze her hand back to let her know just how much.

"Not as much as I love you. Now tell me how is business going for you and Sierra."

"It's going great. We just got our biggest contract to date. W & S Interior Design won the bid to design the additional children's wing in the hospital, once it's constructed."

"Oh my God, Whitney! I prayed your company would get it. Ain't God good?" she asks with a candid smile that shows all of her teeth.

"All the time," I reply and we laugh. I pick up the napkin to wipe my mouth. "I'll be right back. I need to use the restroom," I say, standing and taking a deep breath. I have to walk right past Hart's table in order to get to the restroom.

Do I speak or do I just pretend he's not there? I decide to keep on walking.

"Excuse me," I say as a woman almost walks into me as she walks out of the women restroom.

"No, pardon me," she replies with a smile. I return her smile and walk on into the restroom and quickly make use of one of the empty stalls. I walk out and over to one of the sinks to wash my hands, looking at myself in the mirror to make sure I don't have any food around my mouth or between my teeth.

Satisfied that I'm well put together, I walk out of the bathroom and smack into the wide expanse of a hard muscular chest. My hands automatically grasp his shirt front to steady myself and his hands immediately surround my waist to keep me from bouncing off his solid frame like a volleyball. I look up into the enchanting green-grayish eyes of Hart Martin.

We just stand there for a few seconds, taking in the sight of one another before saying one word. The pure masculine scent of his cologne accosts my nostrils. It's a delicious mixture of lavender, bergamot and a hint of citrus orange, which gives off a Mediterranean aura. It leaves a mesmerizing effect on my heart's rhythm…

"Ahem," Hart clears his throat and brings me out of my dreamy haze. "Hi," he says with a sexy grin.

"Hi," I reply softly and bite my lip nervously.

Hart's eyes go straight to my lips and a hint of something I can't recognize flares to life in his eyes. Then he looks into my eyes again before speaking. "I saw you walk past my table and I thought you would've stopped and spoke to me," he says with disappointment in his eyes.

"I saw you had a date and I thought it would be awkward if I interrupted the two of you," I state with honesty.

"I don't care where I'm at, or who I'm with, I want you to always greet me when you see me. Is that understood?"

I'm shocked by his forwardness, as I stand there mesmerized by the man that Hart has become. His hands squeeze my waist to reaffirm that he means what he says. A sigh of satisfaction escapes my lips. "I understand," I reply, wanting to say more but, with my hand still gripping his shirt, I'm at a loss of something more meaningful to say. "Ah, I guess I better let you get back to your date. I don't want to keep my mother waiting either."

"I thought that was your mother. You look just like her and you both are stunningly gorgeous," he compliments me. The way his eyes twinkle with delight lets me know that his compliments are sincere.

"Thank you," I say, tearing my gaze away from him and trying to step away but his hands still have my waist deadlocked in an intimate grip. "Enjoy your lunch date," I say, as a reminder to us both that there is another woman sitting in this restaurant waiting for him to return.

"Before you go, will you answer just one question for me?" he says, ignoring my statement about his lunch date.

"I will if I can."

"Why haven't you called me to meet up for coffee?"

My eyes cast down to the floor. Honestly, I don't have an answer. It's not like I didn't want to see him again. Hell, I'd been struggling with whether or not to call him and set up a coffee date since I saw him. "I guess I've been so busy with work," I finally answer.

"That's understandable. I've been kicking myself ever since I saw you that night for not getting your phone number. Can I have it now?"

"You said you had one question," I jokingly reply as I try to make light of his question and the fact that his hold on me is heating me to my very core. I can't help but feel oddly awkward that he's asking for my phone number and he's already on a date. "Why do you want my phone number if you already have a girlfriend?" My eyes gesture back out to the restaurant, where the strikingly beautiful woman he's dating is sitting and probably wondering where he is by now.

He looks uncomfortable for a moment but his eyes never leave mine. "Sabrina and I haven't been dating for long. I never lied to her and told her that she was the one for me. She knows we aren't exclusive and that she's free to date other people, just as I am. I just haven't found anyone worth my time since I started dating her. And I've never really wanted to date anyone else, until I met you again."

I release his shirt and quickly and walk off before he can say anything else. Before I turn the corner leading away from the restrooms, I turn around and say, "770-454-7744. That's my cell."

I pass by the table where Hart's date is sitting. I glance at her briefly to see that she's busy admiring herself in her compact mirror. I retake my seat at the table with my mother. "I'm sorry I took so long. I took care of the bill while I was gone," I tell her.

"No problem, sweetheart. While you were away, I got a call from the hospital. Janice, a co-worker of mine's, baby is running a fever and she can't come in and I'm going in to work her shift in just a little bit."

"But you work too many hours through the week to be working on a Saturday too. I had planned for us to spend the day together. I wanted us to get mani and pedi together too," I pout. "Come on, ma. It's your off day."

"I know, but I'll have to take a raincheck, baby. Next time, lunch is on me. You finished eating?" she asks looking at the half eaten food on my plate. I can tell that she's ready to leave as soon as possible.

"Yes," I answer, having lost my appetite anyway.

"What are you going to do with the rest of your day?" she asks as we get up to leave the restaurant.

"I'm not sure. Maybe I'll rent a movie on Netflix or watch a movie on LMN," I reply as I look back once at Hart. His eyes meet mine and he's looking at me as if he wants to exit the restaurant with me. I look away and return my attention to my mother.

"Okay then. If I get a break, I'll call you later," she says and places a kiss on my cheek before getting in her car and taking off. I watch her merge into the traffic before walking over to my car and getting in.

"Here's to another Saturday with nothing to do," I say as I drive down the busy highway towards my apartment building and wonder how long it will take before Hart calls me.

Chapter 6

HART

The next morning, I finish up my morning jog and stop to pick up my Sunday newspaper before running up the steps of my seven-bedroom, five-bath, and two-half-bath Devereaux home on Lakefront Drive. The first floor consists of a wraparound deck off the back porch, a great room, foyer, nook, kitchen and the entrance to a four-car garage. Looking around my home, I feel a sudden urge to hear Whitney's voice. But not before I take a shower and wash away the sweat I worked up from my run.

I take the stairs two at a time leading up to my master bedroom. Somehow, I'm still on a high from reconnecting with Whitney. I walk leisurely to the shower and adjust my water temperature just right. It doesn't take the room long to fill with steam as I step under the refreshing spray. I take comfort in the way the water beats against my flesh.

My mind begins to swirl with thoughts of Whitney standing before me in the shower as naked as the day she was born. My cock hardens instantly at the thought of how she has maintained her gorgeous glow all of these years. She's even more beautiful than I remember, and I remember her being the best looking girl in our class. What made her beauty run the deepest was that she never once treated me like I was the pimple-faced dork that I was. I've loved her spirit for years, and I've lived for the moment that I would reconnect with her.

I take the wash cloth and liberally squeeze Victor Cruz's Go-to shower gel on it before scrubbing my body in circular movements. The incessant spray of water from the triple rotating showerhead casts me in a mist of heated sexual euphoria as my soapy washcloth finds its way to my hard shaft to give it a firm squeeze. "Mmm," my head falls back under the spray of water as I begin to slide my hand up and down as I jerk myself off.

My veins pump with the great flow of blood, the hardness to my cock increases. I can feel the intenseness setting into my hard caress. As the wetness stimulates my swollen gland, I imagine I'm deep inside of Whitney's slick heat, while she writhes beneath me and claws at my back, leaving her mark. That first wave hits and I know I'll cum real soon. I ease off a little, letting it thump, pulsate, and dwindle. The urge is still vibrating, but I mustn't touch it for a few seconds.

I tease the shaft a little, letting my hand slide further towards my scrotum. My balls jump to the sensation and I relish in the smoothness of how I imagine her snug slit to feel. Carrying my stroke back to the tip, I start to jerk it again, but this time faster…much faster. There's a long surge running through me, one that won't stop. It is so damn irresistible. I try not to, but the excitement takes over and the rhythm has me mesmerized. I grit my teeth.

"Shit," I grunt out as I spill my seed to mix with the water as it swirls and washes down the drain. The rest dissolves in my hand. I wash it off with soap and get out of the shower. Slipping into a pair of khaki cargo pants and a dark green Gandy tee shirt, I feel rejuvenated.

I walk over to pick up my cell from the dresser. I scroll through my contacts until I get to Whitney's name and press "Call."

"Hello?" she answers as if she's been sleeping. My cock springs to life again at the sound of her throaty voice.

"Hi Whitney. This is Hart. I hope I didn't call you too early."

"No, not at all," she says. I can hear her moving about as if she's sitting up in bed. I wonder how she looks first thing in the morning. I wonder if her hair is all tousled or if she wears one of those scarf type things on her head like the women on television.

"Good. It's good that I didn't wake you, that is."

"No, you're fine, Hart."

I smile at the way she says my name. "I was wondering…if you're not doing anything today, would you be interested in having lunch with me? I can throw a couple steaks on the grill and we can either sit around the pool or out on the back deck while we eat. Or, we could go to a restaurant. Wherever you will feel more comfortable." I can feel myself rambling. I rub the back of my neck to quell my tension for her answer as I hold my breath.

There's a moment of silence before she answers. A moment that feels like forever. "I'd really like that, Hart," she finally says, and she actually sounds pleased to accept my offer.

"I'm happy to hear that, Whitney." I release the breath that's trapped in my lungs and give her my information. "My address is 2144 Lakefront Drive. You take I-75 to the Red Top Mountain Road exit. That will lead you straight here. You'll see the signs for Lakefront Drive, but if you have any problems, call me," I say, feeling myself become protective of her in a way that I have never felt for Sabrina. It actually pains me to think of her being lost or stranded.

"Got it. What time do you want me?" she says, bringing me back to our conversation.

I want you now, my mind screams out my neediness. I have to adjust my pants for my growing bulge over the implication of her words. *Could this woman turn me on anymore?* I think, even though rationally I know her words are innocent.

"Ah, I meant what time do I come for lunch?" she asks again after my lengthy silence.

"You can come right now," I answer her honestly. I really can't wait to have her in my presence again.

"It's only eight thirty in the morning. Will eleven thirty be okay?" she laughs as she says this.

I know this sounds poetic and maybe even a bit sappy. But the sound of her laughter is like dandelions blooming in summertime as it blossoms more and more under a clear blue sky. The sweet tinkling sounds vibrates through my heart, leaving a trail of precious diamonds behind. I can wait a thousand years just to hear her laughter and a thousand more if I could. I delight in being the cause of this mystical sound and will give anything to make her laugh all the days of her life.

Damn Hart, where are all of these thoughts coming from? I temper myself. I don't want to come off overly strong because I don't want to run her away. "Eleven thirty will be great. And like I said, call me if you have *any* trouble finding the place."

"I definitely will, Hart. I'll load it into my GPS to be on the safe side."

"Okay, I'll see you then, beautiful," I say before we end the call.

I turn and walk out of the room and head back downstairs to my kitchen. I have two steaks that need thawing before she gets here. Everything needs to be perfect for the woman I never would've guessed in a million years would be coming to my home.

Chapter 7

WHITNEY

"Hart Strong just asked me to lunch!" Excitement runs rapidly through my body as I say this to my empty room. The sound echoes off the walls, making my lunch date sound even more exciting. I get up out of bed and go over to my closet. I have to find the perfect thing to wear, where I'm classy and definitely sexy.

The phone rings, jarring me out of my search of the perfect outfit. I look at the caller ID and note that's it's Sierra. Wait until I tell her about Hart…

"Hey, girl. What's up?" I say with a smile in my voice.

"I'm just up getting ready to drive to drive to Auburn. I promised mom and pops that I'd come to dinner today. I have to drive back home right after. That's why I'm getting such an early start."

"Be sure to tell them that I send my best regards."

"I sure will. What do you have planned for today?"

"Nothing much," I smile and sit back against the bed's headboard.

"You are so boring. You know that? You should come with me. You can keep me company on my drive back tonight," she says.

"Nah, I can't go," I say, teasing her.

"Why can't you go? You just said that you don't have any plans."

"Oh, I did say that, didn't I?" I giggle.

"Whit, what are you laughing at? You're sounding mighty sneaky and tight lipped right now."

"Ha, I'm just messing with you," I say, unable to hold out any longer. "Guess who just called and invited me to lunch?"

"Who girl, who?" Sierra asks, sounding like a hooting owl.

"Hart Strong," I say in a nonchalant voice, although I'm feeling just the opposite.

"Not that tall, yum-yum, eat 'em up white man from the mixer a couple of weeks ago?" she says as more of a question.

"Ding, ding…you are correct." I laugh from my own silliness.

"You must have finally gotten the nerve to call him."

"Nope, he just called me a few minutes ago. As a matter of fact, I saw him yesterday when my mother and I went to lunch at Rathburn's and he asked for my number."

"Ooh, I love me some Rathburn's. But getting back to seeing him at the restaurant, tell me what happened and how did you feel seeing him again? Because you ate him up with your eyes at the mixer."

"I did not," I deny and suddenly I notice how affectionately I'd bit my lip afterwards.

"Yes, you did, but that's neither here or there. Just tell me what happened when you saw him again yesterday."

"Like I said, I was having dinner with my mother. In walked Hart right by my table with the most strikingly beautiful woman. Girl, she could have just walked off a runway and into Rathburn's. She sat there with a little bitty salad, barely pecking at it. You should have seen it."

"Oh, so he's into those types, huh?" she questions.

"I guess so," I reply, feeling my mood plummet when I think of Hart and his choice for a girlfriend. I definitely didn't fit into that mold of a woman.

"But, you said he asked for your phone number. He must not be all that into the woman he was with to do something like that, and while she was in the restaurant too."

"I suppose so, but..." I start to speak about him being out with another woman again, but Sierra cuts in.

"Then he invites you to lunch today. Hmm, I definitely will say he's into you, Whit."

"The way I see it, I'm just going to go and have lunch with someone I used to go to high school with. I'm not going to get my hopes up or try to make it more than what it is. Besides, you know I'm not the one to come in between anyone and their woman. I will respect his relationship," I say.

"Is he married?"

"No."

"Well then, what the hell are you talking about? He's free game. I'd be willing to bet that supermodel lady wouldn't give you the same respect if the tables were turned," Sierra says, getting me straight. "Hey Whit, I just checked the time. I got to go, if I want to get ahead of this morning traffic. But I want to hear all about your lunch date tomorrow."

"Okay, I doubt I have that much to tell, but I'll report back tomorrow. Drive safely, sis," I reply and end the call, after we say our goodbyes.

I return my attention to my closet in search of something presentable to wear for my first lunch date with Hart. I decide on a white eyelet short top that stops at my midriff and match it with a pair of striped signature laced shorts. I lay out my clothes before walking into the bathroom to take care of my morning rituals, including a much needed steamy shower.

Chapter 8

WHITNEY

My cell rings just as I merge onto Hart's turnoff leading to his home. I'm running about thirty minutes behind schedule because of the traffic. Plus, I needed to stop for gas, since I had forgotten to refill my tank on Friday.

"Whitney?" Hart's deep, hypnotizing voice greets me.

"Yes?" I answer as a tingling feeling starts at my nape and travels down my spine.

"Where are you?" His voice is calm, but laced with concern.

"I'm about three minutes away. I'm sorry I didn't call to let you know I would be a little late. I needed gas," I explain.

"No problem, I just want to make sure you're not lost and in need of my help."

"You're sweet, I appreciate your concern. But no, everything is fine. I'll see you in a few minutes."

"I can't wait to see you again," he says before disconnecting the call.

Nervousness threatens to creep up my spine, when I pass a mailbox with Hart's address on it. *I'm really about to drive up Hart Martin's driveway,* I think as I turn onto the long, winding pavement leading up to his house. Hart is standing on his front steps waiting for me.

Oh, just look at him standing there looking all sexy and whatnot. What the hell am I thinking coming to his house the first time he asks me out? My thoughts run rapid as I emerge nervously from my car.

"Hello, Whitney," he greets me with a big smile on his face.

"Hi," I return with an uneasy smile.

"Please, don't be nervous. This may seem unorthodox for a first time lunch dates, but you aren't a stranger to me, even if it's been years since we saw one another. I promise I'm not a serial killer, rapist or any of those other things. Besides, I have a nosy, older neighbor that's watching us like a hawk right now. If you'll slowly turn around you'll see that she's pretending to water her lawn, even though she has someone to do that for her."

I slowly turn around and sure enough a little old lady with slightly stooped shoulders and graying hair is looking in our direction.

"Trust me, she'll be looking out of her window all day to see what time you leave," he says with a teasing tone to his voice. I feel his breath on my shoulder, when he yells, "Hello, Ms. Beasley. How are you this afternoon?"

"Good afternoon Hart," replies the little old lady as she grabs at the fabric of her oversized floral gown. "Who's your visitor?" she asks straight forward. She isn't trying to hide her nosiness, as she peers at me behind the wire rimmed spectacles on her nose.

"This is Whitney, an old, dear friend of mine," he says with a friendly tone.

"She's a pretty young lady," Ms. Beasley remarks as she shields her eyes from the brightness of the beaming sun with her hand over her forehead, making no effort to hide that she's trying her best to get a good look.

"Hello and thank you, Ms. Beasley," I say, waving. I'm relieved by Hart's teasing words.

"Come on, let's go inside before she says anything else," he urges me up the steps towards his front door. "Before you know anything, she'll talk you into coming in for coffee, and I refuse to give her a chance to steal my lunch date," he teases. "Have a good day, Ms. Beasley," he calls out to her before we enter his home. He closes the door behind us to give us privacy from his neighbor's prying eyes.

"She looks sweet and harmless," I say once inside and laugh from his earlier comments.

"She is," he cracks a wide smile and I notice how his eyes crinkle adoringly when he smiles. "She also makes the best cranberry chutney cookies that you've ever tasted. Yummy," he adds, rubbing his stomach.

"I love cranberry chutney cookies. My mother gave me the recipe for hers when I went away to college. I make them especially during Thanksgiving and Christmas."

"Maybe you can make me some, sometimes."

He leads me through his spacious home and I notice his high, vaulted ceilings and a traditional wood burning fireplace with built-in bookcases on either side.

"Maybe," I agree and make a note to bake him a batch of cookies in appreciation of him inviting me over for lunch. "Oh, my God. I love your fireplace. Did you build it yourself?" I ask.

"You really like it?"

"Yes, it's unique. I've never seen anything like it," I say, as I walk over and run my hand across the bricks.

"I designed and built it as well as this house," he says with a bit of pride in his voice.

"It's beautiful," I state, meaning every word.

"Thank you. I'll give you a tour of the rest of the house after we eat lunch, if you want."

"Thanks a lot, I'd like to see the rest of your handiwork," I reply as he leads me through an elegant kitchen and out a door that leads to his back deck.

I gaze over the nestle of trees and neatly-trimmed greenery of the lawn. I look out at the lake. The sun displays ripples on the water, as the brightness from the sun sets a picture-perfect scene that's most colorful in nature's beauty. I can see a fish jump out the water and splash back to safety in the distance.

"Did you see that?" I point as the rivulets of water circle inward.

"There are plenty of trout out in the lake," he smiles. "Do you fish?"

"Ah, no."

"You've never been fishing?" he asks in wide-eyed disbelief.

"No," I reply looking into his eyes. "Fishing isn't exactly on my bucket list."

"We must change that. That's my boat out there," he says pointing at a mid-sized boat anchored below. There's also a walkway that leads out into the water. "I'll take you fishing soon," he states as if it's a fact.

"Will I have to touch mushy worms and stuff? Because if I do, I want no part of it." I visibly shudder at the thought.

"No, we won't have to use live bait," he chuckles as he looks down into my eyes. "I use Swimbait Green Tiger fishing lures for trout," he explains patiently.

"Oh, that jiggly plastic like things," I reply, still not warming up to the whole being one with nature idea.

Hart throws his head back and laughs at my comment. "Yes, Whitney. 'That jiggly plastic like things'." I join in on his laughter after hearing a repeat of my words. "Let's have lunch, shall we? You can wash up over there," Hart says, pointing to a free-standing sink that's in a small area with the amenities of a kitchen built onto the deck.

"Very nice," I say as we walk over to wash our hands.

"Thanks. Have a seat and I'll get our steaks and baked potatoes that are warming on the grill. The salad plates are already on the table. I hope Pinot Noir, is okay to drink," he says speaking of the wine that's already chilling in an ice bucket on the table.

"Wine is fine. I can only have one glass since I will be driving."

"Understood," he replies as he brings our steak and baked potato on two plates. He places mine before me. He sits directly across from me with his own. "Help yourself to the salad," he urges me and I do.

He stretches his hands out on the table palms up. I look at him and smile before I place my hand into his. He bows his head to bless our food before we begin to eat. *Wow, this man seems too good to be true.*

"So, tell me Whitney, what have you been up to since I saw you last?"

"That would be graduation day in 2006, right?

"Right," he agrees.

"After graduating high school, I went into an Interior Degree Program at the Arts Institute in Atlanta and got a BFA. That's where I met my best friend and business partner, Sierra Washington. She was my dorm roommate from Alabama. During college, we both interned for Perkins and William's Designing Firm. They're the best in the business and we learned a lot from them. After graduating college, they offered each of us jobs. We ventured out two years ago, taking a chance at our own business, W & S Interior Design. It was a struggle at first and still is. But I find satisfaction in having our own business and at the end of the day, it is so worth it."

"Wow, I'm really proud of your accomplishments. Starting a business is hard as hell, even with the right backing. You have to build up a reputable name for yourself before prospectors will start to take you serious."

"Exactly. This food is so good by the way. You're a great cook."

"I'm glad you're enjoying it." He gives me another dazzling smile that causes wetness to seep into my panties. I squeeze my thighs together to soothe my throbbing clit. *He has a girlfriend, Whitney. He's off limits.* I try to reason with myself.

Damn, I haven't had sex in the seven months since Tony and I broke up, and my womanly needs are internally screaming as I take in his effortless charm. I hope Hart isn't picking up on my desires. The thought of Tony quickly shifts my thoughts from that train wreck of a relationship I would've avoided had I known. I shake my head slightly to clear my mind of him and focus on my conversation with Hart. Tony no longer deserves to take up space in my brain.

"So, catch me up about you. You were always so smart in school in every subject. I always thought you would be a doctor or a scientist," I admit to Hart.

"Nah, although I was good in all of my subjects, I've always loved to build things with my hands. I guess you can say that I had a lot of time on my hands as a kid, since I couldn't play sports. But I built things instead—dog houses, bird houses. I even built a friend of my family's daughter a playhouse once when I was sixteen years old," he reveals to me.

"That's admirable, Hart. I can see you're very talented and it's my loss that I didn't get to know you better growing up," I say with regret in my tone.

"We're getting to know each other now. That's all that matters to me."

A blush grows to my cheeks from the acuteness in his fiery eyes. I nervously take a sip from my wine. I can't believe the effect he's having on me. "Did you go to college?" I ask him, to change the subject.

“I won a full ride to U of CO. The University of Colorado has one of the best Construction and Engineering Management programs in the country. I graduated in three years with all honors.”

“That’s admirable, Hart.”

He shrugs it off as if his accomplishments are nothing to brag about. “I just worked hard and studied even harder. I’m very focused when it comes to something I want,” he says before picking up his wine glass and taking a sip. He peers over the glass and into my eyes as he drinks.

“Being focused and driven are great traits when it comes to business. I read about your construction company in Forbes’s magazine,” I admit that I’ve done my research on Hart Martin and his impressive construction business.

“It was an honor to grace their magazine. They really made me look good,” he says with a humble smile. “After graduating from the university, I had a great start. I never had to really work for anyone else. My grandfather left me more than enough inheritance to start my company from the ground up. In that regard, I’m very blessed to have that money waiting for me when I finished college. May I offer you anything else?"

"Yes, that is a blessing. And no, everything was delicious. Thank you, but I can't possibly eat another bite, even if I tried."

"You're very welcome. Let me clean off the table and I'll give you the tour of the house that I promised you earlier."

"Great, but let me help you cleanup."

"I wouldn't hear of you lifting a finger. You're my guest—"

"So, what? My mother raised me right," I say, before standing to pick up our plates. I leave him to get the rest as I walk off towards his kitchen. I can hear him laughing as he follows behind me.

"What's so funny?" I peer over my shoulder and ask.

"You are beautiful Whitney…You are." He shakes his head from side to side. "I can also see that you are one stubborn woman."

"Do you have a problem with that, Mr. Strong?" I pretend to frown at him before placing the dishes in the sink.

"No problem. I like a bit of spiciness in a woman."

"I see," I said biting my lip. "Is the woman I saw you with at lunch yesterday very spicy too?"

Hart laughs again at my choice of words. My mouth grows into a pout. Actually, I want to know more about the woman he's dating. I don't have time to play heart games with anyone, including Hart.

"I'm sorry," he says as we rinse and place dishes into the dishwasher. "No, Sabrina is not spicy. She happens to be very bland," he answers with a straight face. "No seasoning, none whatsoever."

I bite back a smile and keep a serious expression on my face. I know this is just my first lunch with Hart, but I feel the need to get a clear understanding of what he has going on with Sabrina out in the open. "Oh, really," I cross my arms to stare at him. "Are you two serious?"

"Like I told you yesterday, we are just dating. I'm not planning on marrying her or anything like that."

"How long have the two of you been dating?"

"For less than a year. Maybe eight months," he replies.

"Eight months is a long time. Sounds serious to me," I say and hump my shoulders. I go back to finishing up the dishes.

"Well, I can assure you that we are not serious and Sabrina knows that. She's all the time asking me where we stand and I tell her that we are only dating. What about you Whitney? Is there anyone special in your life?" Hart asks. This time, he is the one to stop and fold his arms across his chest, while he bestows his scrutinizing gaze on me.

"No, if there were anyone special in my life, I wouldn't be here with you. I'm a very loyal woman," I state with directness.

His eyes light up. "So, you're telling me that you are completely single?"

"Correct. But you're not," I say to smother any ideas sparking in his mind about us hooking up. I'm not playing second to another woman, and I damn sure am not about to be foolish enough to think that he's going to just leave her high and dry after eight months of dating.

"I'm not married, Whitney. Do you see a wedding ring on this finger?" he asks, holding up his hand for me to see.

I don't see a ring. But I notice his hand is big, strong and has a few nicks and scrapes on it. Otherwise, his nails are neatly trimmed and clean. The nicks and scrapes attest to the fact that he has worker's hands. I imagine how his big, long fingers would feel against my flesh. I flush inwardly. I really like him, but it's fruitless for me to be having these thoughts. *Damn, why does he have to be taken?*

"I don't see a wedding ring but that's doesn't mean you're not committed, Hart," I say and almost melt, when his eyes plea for me to believe his words and not what I saw at the restaurant. "Listen, I gave almost two years to my last boyfriend. Invested myself really. In those two years, he was also dating someone else. The other woman he married. All I got was a broken heart," I say, feeling disgusted at naivety at the situation. "So, I'm not willing to deal with anyone who's dating another woman."

"I'm so sorry," Hart says with a look of concern on his face. "I could never string someone along in such a way."

I don't mean to, but I fume over his last statement. I mean, what does he mean he could never string someone along in such a way, when that's exactly what he is doing to Sabrina? After eight months, I'm sure she thinks that they're serious, just like I thought me and Tony were serious. Poor girl probably has wedding plans and everything written in a tablet somewhere. I hate to think of Hart in this way, but he's probably no better than Tony. It's time that I bow out of this lunch date. It was fun, while it lasted.

"Hart, thank you for lunch. I really enjoyed catching up with you, but I don't think it's a good idea for me to be having lunch, coffee, or any other kind of date with you as long as you're seeing someone else. I should go," I say retracing my steps towards the front of the house to the front door. I pick up my handbag and reach for the doorknob.

Hart is right behind me every step of the way. His hand covers mine before I turn the doorknob. "Whitney."

He pulls my hand away from the doorknob. He then places his hands on each of my shoulders. His gaze lures mine to his. "I won't pretend to know how much this Tony guy hurt you. And, it may be too soon for me to say this, but I really like you and always have. I don't think we reconnected by chance. I think it was destiny that let us meet again. If it takes me stopping dating to get to know you better, then I will do what I have to do to meet your standards. Give me a chance to handle my business, but don't write me off just yet, beautiful."

I search Hart's eyes. There's no deceit lurking in their depths. "You can call me when you are truly free and we'll talk then," I finally say.

"Thank you." He lets me go and opens the door for me. "I appreciate you coming to have lunch with me, Whitney. I enjoyed your company, and I'll definitely be calling you soon," he says.

I nod my head before turning to walk out the door. I walk down the stairs and unlock my car door and get inside. I take one last look at Hart standing outside his doorway. He lifts his hand in a farewell wave before I start my car and drive away.

I tell myself that did the right thing. As much as I want to know more about Hart Strong, I won't go through what I did with Tony. I don't ever to be blindsided by another man again. My heart could never take such mishandling again. And I wouldn't dare put another woman through what I went through with Tony.

Chapter 9

WHITNEY

This week has started off really busy. It's getting progressively busier by the minute. Sierra and I are supposed to be working, but I'm thinking about Hart Strong. I just can't help it. He's infiltrates my thoughts during my wake and sleeping hours.

"I know you're joking," Sierra says. I'm finally telling her about my lunch date with Hart over a week ago.

"No, I'm not joking. I haven't heard from him since I left his house. He said he was going to call me, but he hasn't, so that's that."

"Maybe he's busy. He does run a successful business, you know."

"Yeah, I thought the same, until I was glancing through the Atlanta Media and saw a picture of Hart and his girlfriend out on a yacht. It appears that she's a celebrity model." I sigh in exasperation. "Maybe he decided to keep seeing her after all, since I told him that I couldn't see him again as long as he has a girlfriend." My heart does a somersault with disappointment. I'm attracted to Hart, but I know this fleeting feeling will go away with time. I can barely get my words out, before Sierra interrupts.

"Girl, I know you didn't tell that man that. You messed up on your first date by giving him an ultimatum like that. Why would you do such a thing, Whit? Never mind," she says, answering her own question. "Tony's ass is the cause of your reasoning. Let me see the picture," she says. I get up and hand the paper over to her. She scans it a bit before returning it to me. "She ain't all that. Skinny heifer," she mutters.

I laugh and return to my seat. I don't have to open my mouth to reply to her statement regarding Tony. She and I both know that my ex-boyfriend is behind my decision not to date Hart. Men will only complicate my life. I have too much work to keep me occupied without thinking about Hart, or anybody else for that matter. Him going this long without contacting me shows his true lack of interest in me anyway. Not hearing from him only makes my decision easier.

"Sierra, I have to meet with C and C jewelers at ten o'clock," I say, changing the subject. "Also, we really need to break down and hire someone to handle all of our appointments. I drove all the way to Marietta yesterday to look at a prospective client's home. Their mini mansion will be good for business, if we get the contract, but it would be good to have someone to do the preliminary work for us."

"Our bid is fair enough for us C and C to make us an offer. And, you're absolutely right about us needing some help in here. We really need someone to run the office while we are out. I'll line up a couple of interviews or call the temp service to see if we can use someone from their pool. You know I have another trip to Auburn planned. My parents' neighbors, Drake and Alyssa Peterson, want me to decorate two rooms in their home. I plan on being there for at least two or three days at the most. Everything I need has already been ordered."

"Oh my God, Sierra. I forgot you told me about that. Drake Peterson, he's the fine ex-football player, right?"

"Yes, honey and those hazel eyes of his mesmerize me to no end. But his wife is beautiful and sweet as she can be. She's the only thing that keeps me from making a play for him myself," she laughs to show she's teasing.

Sierra suddenly sneezes.

"Bless you," I look up from the computer at her.

She squeezes the bridge of her nose, trying to ward off another sneeze. "Thanks Whit. I hope I'm not coming down with a cold. The weather is changing; fall will be here before you know it. Sorry for running out on you for three days, but I promised the Peterson's before checking with you or our schedule," she apologizes.

"No reason to apologize, honey. We will just have to juggle some things around and try to make it work out for us. I'm sure we can." I rub the side of my temple thinking about the mounting workload. I don't need a migraine to slow me down.

"I'm going to get us someone to handle the front desk for us right now," Sierra says.

"Great," I start to say when I feel a presence before it enters the doorway.

“Hey.” Hart stands in the doorway of W & S office with a large bouquet of red roses in his hand.

I look over at Sierra. She sends me a quick look, but she can’t say anything. She’s on the telephone with the temp agency.

“Hey,” I say, getting up from my desk to meet him at the door. “Let’s go out front.” I walk out the doorway and he follows me to the front reception area.

“Are you available to talk?" he asks me with devotion in his eyes.

“Now isn’t a really good time for me. I have an appointment in less than an hour and it’ll take me at least thirty minutes to get where I’m going,” I inform him.

I cross my arms across my chest. It pushes my breasts together. His eyes follow the movement and linger on the deep cleavage put on display by the low cut of my blouse.

“These are for you.” He tries to hand over the fragrant flowers to me.

“I don’t want them. Give them to your girlfriend,” I tell him.

“I don’t have a girlfriend anymore,” he states with frankness.

“I haven’t heard from you since I left your home over a week ago and you’re going to waltz in here with roses and inform me you don’t have a girlfriend. I don’t believe you,” I simmer with a slow burning anger.

“It’s true, I don’t have any reason to lie to you.”

“I don’t have time for this nonsense,” I mutter. “Stay right there. I’ll be right back.” I retrace my steps and march back to my office. Sierra is just hanging up the phone when I enter.

“What does he want?” she whispers.

“I won’t be long.” I hold up my finger to her indicating I won’t be but a minute as I reach for the article on my desk. My heels clack on the tile floor as I walk back out to where Hart is waiting.

“Here,” I hand him over the paper.

“What’s this?” he asks looking at the newspaper in my hand.

“Look at it,” I reply.

He takes the paper from my hand and frowns. "I don't see why this should make you angry with me. This was business, not what you think it is."

"This doesn't look like business to me. You have on swimming trunks and she has a skimpy ass bikini. How is that business?"

"Trust me, it is."

"Well, I need to go," I say looking at my slim wristwatch. "I don't have the time to talk anymore. I have a business to run."

"True, but you have choices," he says with a sneaky smile. His greenish-grey eyes narrow and his teeth flash white against his tan skin.

"I don't like that look, Hart, and I don't have time for games," I glance impatiently at my watch again. "What are you suggesting my choices are?"

"Well, I just so happen to be off work for the entire day. I can take you to your meeting."

Surprised by his offer, I give him a strange look. "Are you telling me that you're willing to drive me across town for my meeting and wait until it's over?"

"That's exactly what I'm saying to you. I'll even take you to lunch afterwards, and then we'll talk about why it took me this long to contact you." His eyes plead for me to say yes. His proposal is too tempting. I've waited a long time to know why he didn't call me back.

"You know what, what the heck? You can be my chauffeur. I hate driving in this traffic anyway. I'm going to get my purse and laptop. Be right back."

"Wait, take these." He shoves the roses in my arms. There's a feeling that comes along with it that I really can't explain. When he hands the flowers to me, I feel something extraordinary. I stand there for a few moments with them in my arms admiring the beautiful bouquet.

"Thank you," I finally say, hiding a smile behind the bunch of roses. A tiny bit of hope rises in my heart. I tell myself that he did take the trouble to look up my business and find my office. Then again, I better wait to hear what his excuse is for taking so long to contact me in the first place.

Chapter 10

HART

I chance a look over at Whitney. She's quietly staring straight ahead as I drive through the mid-morning traffic. I smile inwardly at the stubborn way she's holding her hands clasped in her lap. Before meeting up with her again, it may have been true that I could've settled with dating Sabrina, but not now. Things change. Now that I've been blessed with the presence of Whitney, there's no way in hell I'll stop wanting her, yearning for her or stop myself from becoming hard as steel every time I think of burying myself into her delectable heat. I would just be prolonging the inevitable if I hadn't broken things off with Sabrina when I did. My beautiful Whitney's words set me free to do just the thing I needed to do all along. Sabrina and I have been just wasting each other's time. Life is too short and precious to settle. I want more out of life. I want something solid…something real. I want to feel complete and I'm going to do everything in my power to pursue all of these things and more with Whitney Martin.

"We're here," I finally say breaking our companionable silence.

"Wonderful," she says. I jump out the car, after finding a parking space, and trot around to open her door. "Thank you," she says.

"You're welcome."

She stands before me shorter, but sexier than I've ever imagined a woman can be. I get a chance to gaze into those fiery eyes, when she asks, "What will you do during my meeting?"

"Don't worry your pretty little head about me. Just go and handle your business, boss lady," I urge her.

"I'm not worrying about you," she replies pursing her berry painted lips. I reach over the backseat to retrieve her laptop bag and hand it to her. She places the strap over her shoulder and walks away without another word.

There's something between us. It's almost electric. I can feel it. I smile as I watch the fit of her straight pencil skirt and how it curves against her ass. The skirt and dressy blouse gives her an air of tailored sophistication.

She suddenly looks back to catch me checking out her ass red handed. I can only smile at her and find comfort that she will soon return.

While she was away, I listen to some music on the radio. I love different genres of music: pop, rock and R&B. Grooving to David Bisbal's "Without You," I find myself in my own world. I wonder if this is actually meant to be.

"Gosh Hart. You're acting so silly." I stroke my hair. My emotions taunt me as I glance around the car. The interior is clean, everything is. I love the smell that lingers in the air long after she's gone. It smells just like her perfume, shampoo, and body spray. The atmosphere is eatable.

The song goes off. I listen to a few more and turn the nob to find some sports. I was sure to get an update on the Braves baseball game. I roll down the window and step outside the car. I look towards the building as the announcer gives a brief highlight and, before I know it, my beautiful lady is walking my way.

"I didn't take too long, did I?" Whitney asks as I lean up against the car comfortably.

"No, not at all," I glance at my Rolex watch. "Your meeting lasted less than an hour. How did it go?" I ask as I help her into the car before going around to get behind the wheel.

"It went great. We have the contract. This year is the best year yet for W & S Interior Designs," she adds with a captivating smile, one that shows more of her features, like the dimple on the right side of her cheek. The flash of something behind those eyes and that irresistible twinkle that glows all around her mesmerizes me to no end. It's like I can see her soul through her illuminating orbs.

"That's great," I reply looking both ways before merging into the afternoon traffic. I must harbor my feelings inside; I don't want to scare her away by coming on too strong, too soon. She deserves to be wined, dined and treated with the utmost respect. "Where do you want to have lunch? Pick anywhere you want," I tell her. It really doesn't matter to me where she chooses to go. I'm willing to give her whatever she wants.

"Hmmm...Let's go to Journey's on Peach Tree. They serve the best chili fries and slaw dogs around."

"Sounds great to me," I reply and take the ramp off I-85.

Thirty minutes later, Whitney and I are seated in a red booth with red and black vinyl menus on the table. There's a napkin holder and a few condiments lined on the side: sugar, ketchup, and salt.

"What can I get you two?" asks the young waitress as she pops her gum loudly.

"I want the slaw dog special with chili cheese fries and a cola to drink. Oh, and hold the onions." Whitney wastes no time in placing her order.

"I'll have the exact same thing she's having," I tell the waitress.

"I'll be right back with yawls orders," she says before gathering the menus and walking away.

Moments seems so damn timeless when Whitney's around. I'm lost for words and happy that I finally get a chance to be in her presence as we make small talk. The waitress returns and shoves two dishes on the table.

"I'm waiting," Whitney looks directly at me as she takes the first bite of her slaw dog.

I know exactly what she means, so I go straight into my explanation which is the truth. "I had to fly to Maine to take care of a problem firsthand on a job, which was contracted out to my company. When fires crop up, either Leo or myself have to be on hand to put them out, so to speak. I was planning to fly in and out in a day or two, but I had to stay for most of the week to make sure everything went according to plan. If you don't believe me, my bags are still in the car. I looked you up and came straight from the airport to see you."

Whitney looks at me with bewitching, alluring brown eyes. I can see indecision and want warring in her eyes. I reach across the table to gather her small hands that she has clasped together on the table into my own. I look deep into her eyes when I speak to her again.

"One thing I want you to know about me is that I'm not going to hurt you. I promise to show you off to my friends every chance I get. Eventually when you're ready to meet my family, you will meet them. Everyone in my life will know that Hart has found the one that he never should have let get away. I just want you to know that

I'm on a mission. I plan to win your heart and, once I win it, it's mine for keeps. You got that, Whitney Martin?"

She sits there speechless for a moment but nods her head up and down. "I, I need to get back to the office," she finally says. "I've already went over my lunch hour."

"I tell you what, lets order Sierra lunch to go," I offer.

"Yes, thank you. You're so kind. She'll like that."

"For you, always," I say, waving for the waitress to come over. I place a to-go order for Sierra and then drive Whitney back to W & S Design. We arrive in no time.

"Thank you so much for the ride and lunch," Whitney says once I see her to the door of her building.

"You're welcome sweetheart. Anytime."

"Call me soon," she says shyly.

"Definitely, I will," I promise her.

She looks up at me before reaching her free hand up and placing it against my cheek. She stands on her tiptoes, so I bend my head for her to place a soft kiss against my cheek. "Bye, Hart and thanks again."

She opens the door and steps inside her building. The beginning of a smile starts on my lips until it's a full-fledged grin by the time I'm in my car amidst heavy traffic. There's nothing in the world that I want more than her now.

Chapter 11

WHITNEY

"Hey Sierra, everything is going great at the office and the new temp you hired is working out great. I'm heading home for the evening. When you get this voicemail, I just want you to know that you don't have to worry about a thing. I have everything under control and caught up on this end. And one more thing," I hurriedly say before the dreaded beep cuts off my message. "Get me an autographed picture of Drake Peterson. Mother loves him. Okay, bye." I end the call just as I pull up at my apartment building.

I park my car and grab the dress from the back seat that I had shopped for during lunch for my date with Hart tonight. I let myself into my apartment and head straight for my bedroom. I don't want to keep Hart waiting when he arrives, so I kick off my heels and discard my clothes on my way to the shower.

I worked extra late so that I wouldn't have any business to worry about. I can be completely free to enjoy my time with Hart. I don't know what kind of plans he has in store, but I'm excited to have another date with him.

We seem to be getting closer and closer with each conversation we have, since he calls me every night. I love to fall asleep to the sound of his voice in my ears. The huskiness of his voice soothes me to sleep at night. Sometimes, I pretend he's lying there with me. His tone is so sensuously deep, more seductive than I can hardly take at times. I crave for him to crawl through the phone and hold me in his arms as he makes sweet love to me, but I dare not voice my salacious thoughts to him. He has been such a gentleman at all times in my presence; I refuse to be the one trying to get freaky. We haven't even had a real kiss yet.

The even better thing is that we have a lot in common. Hart believes in punctuality and so do I. We even talked about money and finances. I'm happy to know he believes in being financially responsible. My parents taught me financial responsibility at an early age and it's still ingrained in me, even until this day. Hart is laid back and I take a more serious approach to life. I welcome that difference because we can balance one another out. He's my yin to his yang…He believes in love and family and so do I. What more can I ask for in a guy?

I step underneath the hot spray of the showerhead. As the first drop of hot water hits my skin, I stand immobile for a bit. The refreshing spray is relaxing with soothing effects. I reach for the herbal, fruity, conditioning shampoo in the caddy and squeeze a dollop onto the palm my hand. I rub my hands together and give my natural hair a good lather before rinsing the suds from my head, leaving it squeaky clean. I pay close attention and reach for the bar of Dove soap to lather every inch of my body before the irresistible feel of the hot water rinses the suds away, leaving my skin smooth and soft to the touch. The thought of Hart's big hands all over my body causes my nipples to perk up and harden as I step from the shower to dry off.

I give my wet hair a vigorous shake as I open my mouth to speak. "What have I gotten myself into with Hart Strong? I'm falling for him faster than I thought was possible."

I clear my mind of those thoughts to quickly warm wand my natural hair so it will be set in time. I slide on a pair of black, silky lace G-string panties and a matching black lace bra before sliding my new Paisley halter print dress over my head. I slip my freshly pedicured feet into a pair of slinky Bowknot high-heeled shoes to compliment my dress. By the time I'm fully dressed, I remove the wand curlers and clips from my hair. My curls brush my shoulders in a bouncy and sexy way that leaves me satisfied with my handiwork.

Hart arrives right on time and knocks on my apartment door. I open the door and his magnetic presence overwhelms me, causing my throbbing pulse to run erratic.

"Oh my God, you're so beautiful," he says standing in the doorway assessing me with his heat-filled gaze, holding a single red rose in his hand. "This is for you," he hands it over to me.

"Thank you, Hart." I blush as I take the rose and bring its fragrant petals to my nose to sniff. "Come in, I have a small vase I can put this in." I step away from the door to allow him to come inside and close the door behind me.

"Your apartment is very nice," he compliments.

"Thanks, but it's not as great as your house." I reach for the small vase on my curio shelf and walk to the kitchen to fill it with water. I place the lone rose into it. "Do you want anything to drink?" I call over my shoulder.

"No," his seductive voice makes me jump nearly out of my skin from fright. I didn't realize he had walked up behind me.

"Sorry," he says, catching the small vase I nearly dropped on the tiled kitchen floor. That would have been a disaster.

"That's okay, great save. I just didn't realize you were this close behind me." I look up into his handsome face as the exotic smell of his cologne assails my nostrils. I bite my bottom lip and clench my hands to keep from grabbing his shirt front and demand that he kisses me properly.

"I love when you do that," he says, sitting the vase down on the nearby bar.

"You love it when I do what?" I ask as our eyes continue to devour one another.

"I love how you bite your bottom lip every time I get this close to you." A shiver runs down my spine from the truth of his words. "Do I make you nervous, Whitney?" He invades my space by moving even closer to me. His body seems to dwarf my kitchen's size.

"Ah, no…" I stutter out before nibbling on my bottom lip again. I glance in the other direction, appearing to be checking on the rose again. It's ridiculous, but I need something to distract me.

Hart harshly sucks in his breath before cupping the side of my face with his large hands. I can feel the callouses on his hands against my cheek. I find it so irresistibly sexy to think about the hard work he puts in right alongside his employees to make his construction company such a success. He's the kind of leader anyone should be honored to work for. He doesn't just give direct orders; he also shows how to follow through on them by doing.

"I've been wanting to do this ever since I first saw you again. I've been restraining myself to keep my hands to myself and remain a gentleman. Forgive me Whitney, if I'm out of line, but I have to do this. I need to do this," his voice trails away as his lips descend upon mine.

Do it already, a voice screams silently through my head.

Harts eyes are intensely locked with my own as the distance between our lips grows shorter. "Hey there beautiful," he says just before he slides one hand down to encircle my waist and press my body against his.

"Hey," I whisper softly. His lips claim mine just as I hoped they would for what seems to be an eternity.

A sigh escapes my open mouth and he swallows it intimately as our breaths merge, our lips and bodies mesh. My hands that hang loosely at my sides find their way around the nape of his neck. My fingers brush against the silky, wavy hair at his hairline. There's a surge of sexual energy running through me.

Our kiss is hot, but then, unexpectedly, his tongue plunges fiercely and deliciously into my mouth to twirl with my own. My nipples bud and press against my lace bra. I'm sure their sharpness can be felt against the soft fabric of Hart's Burberry Brit button down shirt.

"Mmmm," I moan lustily under the tutelage of his fiery kisses. He takes this moment to slowly pull away. My puckered lips move forward with an attempt to bring his lips back against mine.

"Ahem," he clears his throat and stands out of my reach to his full height. "We better go. If we keep this up, the whole night I have planned for us will be ruined, because we'll be late for our reservation."

Let it be ruined…let it be damned, I think. For once, my mind and body are on the same page, screaming for Hart to take me now. I want to say but don't.

"Okay, let me grab my clutch," I say instead, walking off towards my bedroom. I check to make sure my cell and keys are inside before walking over to the bedroom mirror to replace the glossy lipstick on my swollen lips.

"You ready?" he asks, when I return.

"Yes," I reply softly, before he opens and closes the apartment's door. The door automatically locks behind us as we make our way to Hart's vehicle. The low sound of jazz music pipes from the cars speakers.

"Where are we going?" I ask.

"I thought we'd go to dinner first, for the first part of our date. I made reservations at Aria's over in Buckhead. I hope that's satisfactory with you."

"Of course, it is." I feel more and more impressed with Hart. Tony never took me to places like that. But he spent a fortune for the woman he married and even took her on a vacation to Aruba, the one he and I had planned on taking during the Summer of 2017. "I've always wanted to go to Aria's but never have," I add.

"I'm glad I'm the one taking you for the first time," he says and reaches over with his free hand to intertwine his fingers with mine. He places our locked hands on his thigh. I can feel the corded muscles in his thigh beneath his dress slacks.

"I'm glad you are too." I swallow the lump that tries to form in my throat and say, "Thank you."

"You're welcome. I hope to make this a date to remember," he says as he pulls in the parking lot of the restaurant and finds a place to park.

He gets out the car to come around to open the door for me, a habit of his that I'm already getting used to. My dress slides far up my thighs as I swing my legs around to stand. I don't miss the heat from his eyes when they land on my brown thighs. He holds my hand during the short walk inside the elegant interior of the restaurant.

"Reservation for Hart Strong, for two," he tells the hostess.

"Right this way." The hostess leads us to an intimate table for two in the dimly lit room. "Your waiter will be with you shortly," she says once Hart has seated me and taken a seat of his own.

"Good evening sir, madam," the waiter says as he approaches our table and pours wine into Hart's glass and waits for him to sample it. Once Hart gives his nod of approval, he fills my glass before pouring more into Hart's glass.

I pick up my glass to take a small sip. Hart's scorching stare is on my face as I sip the wine. I blush and a shy smile forms on my lips from his hot gaze. The sweltering look in his eyes causes my panties to become instantly saturated.

A warm smile forms on his lips as we watch one another without saying a word. Flames from the candlelight dance intimately between us. I enjoy the way he's watching me and the way his eyes caress my face, neckline, and even the slope of my shoulders. I feel like a kitten in his cave. If just his gaze can cause this much turbulence within me, then his mouth, lips, and hands will surely ruin me for all others. I have no doubt of this.

"I will be back with your orders," the waiter says before he walks away. The waiter's words cut into my line of thought. I bite my lip again to ward off any more salacious thoughts that try to enter my mind.

"I hope you don't mind but I had our meal planned when I called for our reservations. That's why I asked you during our last phone conversation if you have any known allergic reactions to certain foods or dyes," Hart says.

"I assumed we were just getting to know each other and the things we liked. You're very thorough, Hart, and very thoughtful."

"I try to be." He flashes me another of his heart warming smiles.

We hardly notice the waiter as he places our plates in front of each of us. Our eyes are feasting on each other. Once that gaze is broken, I note the plate contains assorted thin slices of cheeses and an array of exotic sweet fruit. I bring a slice of cheese to my lips and he watches me with a look of hunger in his eyes.

"Ummm, Hart, this cheese is very good. You should try it."

"I want to taste yours," he states, and my panties gush with my desire again. At this rate, I'm going to have to change my underwear or remove them completely.

"Here." I reach towards his mouth and feed him the bit of cheese I'd just bitten.

"Mmmm, it is delicious." He picks up a juicy strawberry and feeds it to me. The juice from the fruit dribbles down my chin. I laugh nervously as I pick up a napkin to wipe it away. "I'm so jealous of that napkin right now. If we were alone, I would be licking the juice off of you." His voice is smooth and low.

My face flushes. Even under the candlelit glow, I know my blush is noticeable. The world stops spinning on its axle as it comes to a complete standstill. Hart and I become lost in our own universe. I hardly even notice when our dinner plates arrive. The flaky fish cooked in tamarind juice is delicious. I go through the methodical act of picking up my fork, placing food in my mouth, and swallowing. All because I'm wrapped up in Hart's remediate stare. I'm savoring everything about him as if I'm appreciating this scrumptious meal. The dinner plates are cleared at some point and a single dessert for two is placed between us. The orange soufflé looks delicious but I'm still full from the meal I hardly remember eating.

"This looks delicious Hart, but you will have to eat this by yourself. I'm stuffed."

"Here, just one small bite, please, then no more," he says picking up the fork and cutting into the light and airy dessert. "Open," he directs me to open my mouth.

I open for him and he feeds me the citrusy dessert. It melts in my mouth like butter, dissolving on my tongue. "Mmmm, it's so good. If I had known you ordered this dessert, I would have saved room for it."

"No worries, beautiful. I will make sure to have your very own dessert delivered to you."

"Hart, you are spoiling me," I say, my heart melting from his sweet gesture.

"Stick with me. You haven't seen anything yet. Are you ready for the second phase of our date? We have fifteen minutes to get there. It's only a short distance from here," he adds.

"Yes, I'm ready," I reply, curious about what the second phase of our date consists of.

My question is answered ten minutes later as we pull up beside Kasey Landon's Beginners Swing Dance Studio.

"Hart, I don't know about this," I say as he leads me inside. "I've never swing danced in my life."

"Neither have I, but it'll be a fun adventure. This will be a first real date of many, I hope." He has a teasing glint in his eyes as he ushers me into the building.

Dancing has never been one of my main qualities, but a girl can groove with her hips. I don't plan to tell

Hart that until we get on the floor. Hopefully, I can get the hang of the swing dance moves quickly.

"Hello and welcome," an older woman steps forward and introduces herself. "I'm Kasey Landon and this is Joel Underwood," she introduces an older gentleman who is tall in stature and has a smile on his face.

"I'm Hart Strong, and this is my girlfriend, Whitney Martin," Hart says with beaming pride.

Did I hear right? Hart just called me his…girlfriend. I immediately become deaf to everything else he's saying. Hart's voice sounds like light mumbling chatter. Unsurmountable joy ricochets through my body from his words.

"Everyone welcome Hart and Whitney to the class," Ms. Landon says.

The other couples smile and gloat at our presence. They welcome us and introduce themselves, as well.

"Okay, before we get started, I want to give a little history about swing dance to the new students. The original Swing era began in the nineteen twenties and thirties. This was a time when the big bands took over the pop culture in America. Swing music has lived on ever since. This helped the evolution of jazz music in the nineteen twenties. Over time, the bands grew smaller and the dance rebranded itself. It became the jitterbug, boogie-woogie, the jive, and the rock and roll, just to name a few," Ms. Landon went on to say.

I find the whole history interesting and the excitement has built inside of me by the time the music begins. Hart and I are well on our way to learning the steps to swing dancing. We have so much fun, dancing through the night. This is the best date I've been out on, ever.

Chapter 12

HART

"Hart, I've never had so much fun in my life," Whitney says as excitement oozes from her every word. "I never want the night to end. Look at the zillions of stars in the sky," she says as she twirls in her high heels and looks up at the luminous night sky.

"Tonight is and has been fun. But you know what's even more incredibly beautiful?" I ask her.

"No." She stops spinning around and stares at me with curious brown eyes. Our hands are inseparable; the magnetic feeling in between us is too real.

I can't hold it back any longer. My emotions spring forth and my lips confess it all. "You are," I state, meaning every word.

Whitney Martin is the most beautiful, delectable and desirous woman I've ever laid eyes on and I've been with many but none can hold a candle to her. With Sabrina, it was all about appearances and having the latest or most stylish material things. She never would have enjoyed a night of dancing, unless we were amongst the rich and famous. Whitney finds joy in the simplest of things. I love her confidence, her smile, her sensuousness, her independence but I find pleasure in her allowing me to do simple things for her.

She smiles at my compliment and bends her head as if she's suddenly shy.

"Don't do that, Whitney."

"Do what, Hart?" Her eyes return to mine as she walks through the doors.

"Don't look away whenever I compliment you. You better get used to it. Because when it comes to you, I'm loaded with them." I chuckle as I open the passenger door of my car and wait for her to get inside.

"Yes, sir," she answers with a giggle. "I will remember that, sir," she teases as I settle behind the steering wheel and start the ignition.

"Tomorrow is Sunday and neither one of us has to work. You said you don't want the night to end…do you mean it, Whitney?"

"I mean it, Hart," she answers with no hesitation.

I need to make myself clear, so there won't be any misunderstandings down the line. "I want to take you home with me. I want to make slow, sweet love to you until both of us are satiated and can hardly move. Do you want the same thing?" My heart beats at an erratic pace while I await her response. She blinks once and stares off into the night. A car passes and she turns back to face me. Her gaze is unreadable and time seems to pause. I watch her lips carefully as she opens them.

"I want the same thing…I have for a while now," she admits.

"I'm glad to hear that. Once I go down this path with you, it'll be you and me and no one else. I don't share someone I love. Never. Ever," I state emphatically.

"I understand," she says as she bites her bottom lip again.

"Damn," I grunt as my cock aches and swells uncomfortably beneath my slacks. Her look of innocence is enough to make me blow a damn gasket.

"Wha—" she begins but I take her hand and place it over my crotch area.

"Feel that?"

Her eyes widen as her eyes follow the placement of her hand. She doesn't say anything at first and I wonder if I've gone too far. Maybe she's not as freaky as I am, but the feeling of her hand against my slacks has me wanting to combust then and there. She slowly eases her hand to my thigh and squeezes it. Everywhere her hand touches, heat settles in that spot. No other words are spoken between us as I drive above the speed limit to my house. What might have taken forty-five minutes, I easily make it in thirty.

"You want anything to drink?" I offer out of politeness, once we enter my home. I hope she says no. I've waited too long to get my first taste of her sweet goodies and I don't want to wait any longer.

"No," she says softly. "I just want you and that's all."

"Shit," I grunt out before scooping her up in my arms and half jogging towards the stairs.

"Wait, put me down, I'm too heavy."

"You are no such thing," I reply taking the stairs two at a time until I arrive at my bedroom door. I use my foot to push it open and walk over to my king size sleigh bed to place her on top of the duvet. I'm glad I decided to leave on a bedside lamp before I left. It dimly lights the room with a warm, inviting glow.

"We need to get you out of these clothes." I reach out to assist her, first grabbing for her shoes.

"No, I got this." She looks at me seductively under hooded eyes.

I watch as she stands up from the bed and slowly bends to gather the hem of her dress and slide it off of her body in a provocative tease. That alludes that she wants more than sex, she wants seduction. She flings her dress at me and I catch it in one hand. I bring the soft lace fabric to my nose to inhale her flowery scent that clings to the material.

My cock twitches as she stands before me in a black lace bra and G-string panties. I throw the dress over the back of a chair and stalk towards her. I have lost all patience. I have to be near her, right now.

I spin her around so her back is against my chest and I lift her slightly so the feel of her well-rounded ass is against my crotch. I look up into the overhead mirror to see the sexy expression on her face. Her mouth is ajar, her tongue sliding along the curve of her lip.

Whitney smiles and arches her back to press the curve of her rear into my crotch. My palms graze over the swell of her hips, then over her soft belly. She trembles slightly and eases back to rest her head against the wide expanse of my chest. I push her back onto the bed and spread her thighs for my scrutiny. I take a mental picture of her, so I will remember how she looks at this moment for the rest of my life.

I kiss her slowly. Our tongues battle for domination as they twirl and plunge into each other mouths. She laces her fingers behind my neck as my hands slide further up her body with an urge to touch her tantalizing breasts.

The overhead mirror attached to the ceiling reveals our reflection. My cock lengthens even more and throbs in anticipation of entering her secret pleasures, even though I'm overdressed.

My fingertips brush and cup each sensitive orb of her cushiony breasts softly, before raking my fingernail over her nipples. Her eyes close and a faint gasp escapes her lips.

"Oh Hart…"

I'm feeling bolder by the minute. I ease my head down to nibble and lick the length of her neckline while gently rolling the peaks of her breasts between my thumbs and forefingers.

Whitney's head flings back on the big fluffy pillows as she cries out my name for a second time. I squeeze her breasts harder into my big hands. They feel so good in my hands. She must be enjoying what I'm doing because her fingers begin to paw desperately at my neckline.

"You're so beautiful," I whisper, hoarsely. One of my hands is still cupping her pliable right breast, my other hand uses this time to travel and explore her stomach area. "I can't wait to touch the inside of your hot walls," I say to her, my voice is etched with passionate thirst.

My fingertips slide down even further between her supple thighs. She sighs as I press my fingertips beneath the black lace of her panties. She is so wet…so very wet. I can feel the moisture on my fingertips. The anticipation drives me insane. I let out an animalistic groan as I dip between her slippery folds. In and out, in and out, I plunge.

"Oh, Hart," Whitney cries out, when my fingers gently but firmly seek out and stroke deeper into her sticky sweetness.

"I want to kiss you here. I want to taste you here," I whisper into her ear.

Whitney's wet heat invites me and urges me to act on my words. Her moans tell me how much she wants and needs it. I love looking up at her in the mirror. Whitney's eyes are still closed. Her chest rises and falls rapidly with her shallow, uneven breaths as she breathes in and out rapidly.

"Yes," she moans and her muscles start to tense up as she nears the pinnacle of an orgasm. My strokes become faster, flicking her stem from side to side. "Yesss…yesss," she screams on a long, drawn-out wail.

"Cum for me, Whitney…let go." I order her as I continuously plunge my fingers into her wetness, strumming her clit until her shivers become controlled. Her eyes gleam and her mouth gasps with exasperation. I can feel her inner thighs clinching my hand in her wanted position.

My barely audible words are all it takes to send her over the edge. I ease off the bed and quickly discard my clothing, before reaching out to cradle her body against my own. She's still trembling from the ferocious convulsions of her orgasm. Her seductive moans subside and her body collapses against my hard body.

"I'm not done with you yet," I grumble into her fragrant, natural hair, before tearing her out of her delicate panties.

She watches me through the slits of her half-closed eyes. I hover over her curvy, delectable body, before covering her body with mine. At the last minute, I remember to protect her as I reach over into my nearby bedside table drawer to remove a condom. I sheath my hard length in latex to make myself ready to love her the way I'm aching to…in the same way she deserves to.

"Take me Hart, do it now." She begs and I about come undone. Shit, it's her affection that drives me now.

I take my time trailing kisses and gentle nips along the inside of her knees, the soft skin of her inner thighs and the flat plane of her stomach. I give each nipple a flick of my tongue before settling between her luscious thighs.

Whitney wraps her arms around my neck and her legs around my waist as she pulls my body closer to her own. "Make love to me Hart. Please don't make me wait any longer." She sighs before my head swoops down to mesh her lips with mine.

I thrust my tongue into her mouth just as my cock plunges into her body. It feels like the earth just shook. Or is it my body quaking from immeasurable pleasure? I close my eyes and keep a steady pace.

The throbbing in my hardness increases with each fiery stroke. A tidal wave of pleasure suddenly washes over me. "Oh, Whitney" I groan hoarsely against her lips. "You feel incredibly hot," I grate out.

I ease out of her to the tip and plunge back with a quick, deep thrust into her with precision. Provocative cries pour from both of our lips. She tightens her legs around my waist and tilts her hips into an upward grind to meet my shaft thrust for thrust, plunge for plunge, and grind for grind. Our bodies collide making a slapping wet sound.

Whitney cries out an orgasm for the third time tonight. Her clutching muscles pulsate around my hard erection. The gratified sound she makes is like the sweetest music to my ears.

"Right there, Hart, right there," she whimpers softly.

She clings tightly to me, gasping and cooing the sweetest of melodies into my ear. Her hot, sweet, sex sounds push me over the cliff and my hot seed fills the latex to the brim. I give my all to this woman that I love, and have loved for years. I express the depth of what I feel for her and hope that she's feeling every bit of what I'm giving to her with my heart, body and soul.

Chapter 13

WHITNEY

Sierra's personal cell phone is continuously chiming from her handbag. I look up from the computer and gaze at her. She's just sitting at her desk staring out the window as if she doesn't hear the ringing sound.

"Sierra, what is wrong with you? You've been acting strange ever since you came back from Auburn three days ago."

"Nothing is wrong. I guess I'm just tired." She sighs.

"You did a great job on the Peterson's two rooms," I say, trying to cheer her up, even though it's the truth. "The pictures you took for our portfolio are great," I add.

"I did do exceptionally well, didn't I?" A small smile flits across her lips, although it's fleeting. A sad look reenters her eyes.

"You know, you can talk to me about anything. We've never kept secrets from one another. Hell, I tell you all of my business, so what's going on?"

"True, we don't keep secrets. It's nothing. Don't worry about me. You never finished telling me about the hot date you had with, Mr. Charismatic," she says, changing the subject. Even though I know what she is doing, I allow her to. But I can't decide whether or not I will tell her how close Hart and I have gotten or not.

"Hart is so romantic, Sierra. He's everything to me," I say as memories flash before my eyes of the night we made love. "He's so considerate and always tries to make me comfortable. I wish he would've walked into my life long ago. It would've saved me from making a fool out of myself with Tony."

Sierra perks her lips at me. "Girl, Tony should have known he was wrong about how things went down between you and him. Any man with a shred of decency would. He was supposed to be on a business trip for TriTek, but he was in Aruba having the wedding and honeymoon of a lifetime. The dream trip he was supposed to take you on next year nonetheless," she says with a roll of her eyes.

"You are so right. It makes me mad every time I think about it. I know dwelling on what Tony did to me will only give him residence in my heart and thoughts. I won't give him that kind of power, any longer," I confess. Hart's brilliant smile as we danced on our first date comes to mind and all traces of Tony leaves.

"That's my girl. I'm so proud of you," she says, just before her cell buzzes again. "Ugh," she grabs her handbag and reaches inside for her phone. She glances at it, before she presses a button and throws it back into her handbag. I wonder what's up with Sierra. She's not acting herself. "Sooo, have you and Mr. Charismatic done the tango yet?" she asks.

"You expect me to tell you my personal business and you won't even tell me who you're dodging on the phone? Uh-uh, I don't think so."

"Be like that then," she says, getting up and carrying a folder over to the file cabinet.

"I'm going to lunch now, if it's okay with you two", says Paula Byrd, our new receptionist.

"That's fine, Paula. Before you go, I just want you to know that you're doing a great job here. We appreciate you," I say, thankful of the load she has taken off of us.

"Thank you, Miss Martin." I give her a hard look. "I mean, thank you, Whitney," she corrects herself and we laugh.

"Enjoy your lunch Paula," Sierra cuts in.

"Do either of you need anything?"

"No," we both reply, before she leaves.

"She is so considerate, isn't she?" I glance over at Sierra. She is staring out the window again.

"Did you say something, Whitney?"

"Nothing that's important."

A bell chimes on the front door in the lobby. Sierra and I look up as Hart walks into the office. "Hi, you two," he says with an easy grin on his handsome face.

"Hello, Hart," Sierra is the first one to speak while a sappy grin appears on my face and I eat him up in his blue chambray shirt and relaxed fit jeans. A pair of tan steel-toe work boots encase his feet. He looks good in a suit, but this work gear is sexy as hell too. My man really looks well in anything he wears.

“You have the most impeccable timing,” Sierra speaks.

“Why do you say that? What’s going on?” he asks as a look of confusion enters his eyes.

“Yeah, I want to know the answer as well.” I give her a hard look.

Sierra hesitates before replying. “I just thought that since you’re here, you can take Whit out to lunch or something.” She’s quick to take the conversation into a different direction.

"As a matter of fact, that’s why I’m here. I only have an hour or so, but I want to spend it with my girl,” he says, looking directly into my eyes.

Hart’s eyes latch onto my lips. He stares at them like he misses them, as if he wants to kiss them. I wouldn’t protest if he did. My cheeks feel as if they are aflame from the heated look in his eyes.

Sierra goes to her desk and sits. She looks at me and then Hart. “I have a suggestion.”

“What’s that?” We both happen to say at the same time.

“There’s a nice hotel down the street. Why don’t you both just get a room and have at it. Sheesh.” She giggles and shakes her head from side to side. “Because if you two keep looking at each other like that, I swear this room will burst into flames,” she fans her face with her hands.

Hart laughs and nods his head in the affirmative. "Well, yes that’s a great idea."

"But I..."

“I’m only teasing, Whitney.” He laughs, but the hot look in his eyes tells a different tale. “What I want to do to you will take much longer than a lunch hour,” he states in a serious tone.

“Oh my...” I suddenly jump up from my seat and walk around the desk to greet my man properly. Professional or not, I grasp his shirt front and pull him towards me. His head bends without resistance as his lips meet mine in a scorching kiss. “Fantastic,” I finally say once I let him up for air. “Now we can go to lunch,” I walk back around the desk to retrieve my purse.

Sierra sits there with her mouth agape as we walk out the door hand and hand. I can't help but giggle at the look on her face. I'm deliriously happy being with the man that I love and there's no way I can hide it.

Chapter 14

WHITNEY

I stand at my bedroom window and watch the darkening sky. In the waning light, I can see trees bend from the strong winds. A flash of lightening zigzags through the sky, illuminating its magnificent skyline.

It is just after six in the evening and, other than the brewing storm, the night causes me discomfort because of the telephone call I received about an hour earlier. I wish I hadn't answered the phone. His voice…Tony's voice brings back too many memories of when I thought everything was perfect between us, but I see clearly now. Our relationship had only been a mirage.

I'm glad I had awakened from my infatuated state of bliss before I'd made an even bigger fool of myself. I've lain in my room and cried many tears over Tony. I'll be dammed if I cry anymore. I should've denied him when he asked to see me again. I should've told him "No" and to "Go to hell", instead of saying I would "think about it." But I guess I want answers. I want to know why he mishandled my heart in the way that he did. Why he up and married another woman without even dumping me first?

I walk through my bedroom to my adjoining bathroom that's decorated in bright pastel colors. I splash my face in cold water to regain my bearings. I jump in fright, when I hear a boom of thunder in the distance. It's loud enough to be heard through my apartment walls.

I don't want to be here alone. I want to see Hart. He always has a way of making me feel better, making me forget that Tony ever existed. Even though he should be calling me in another hour, an idea dawns on me. I'm going to surprise him at his house tonight. This will be a first for me, since I'm usually not one for spontaneity. I guess Hart has been good for me. With him, I think I've lighten up a lot. He's bringing out the best in me. We complement one another in a good way.

I decide to beat the storm and hurry to my closet to get my overnight bag. I add a change of clothes for work tomorrow, a night shirt, and a change of underwear. I already know Hart has extra toothbrushes available for me to use. I dash out to my car and look up at the sky. The clouds gathered above are growing darker. There's a rumble in the sky, but so distant that I can barely hear it. To make matters worse, the lightning flashes are growing closer together.

Maybe, this isn't the brightest idea I've ever had…Too late, I tell myself. I pull out of my parking spot and nose my way on the interstate towards Hart's home.

Thirty minutes later, I park in Hart's driveway. I don't see his car or truck but think both are probably in his garage. By the time, I grab my overnight bag and rush towards the front door, heavy raindrops begin to fall. I run and make it towards the shelter of his porch, just as the thunderstorm unleashes its fury on the world.

Hart opens the door after I have rung the doorbell about four times. I know he isn't asleep because he never goes to bed this early. He stands in the doorway stoic and silent, before a look of surprise followed by wariness enters his eyes. So many emotions flit across his face in such a short time that I become worried.

"Aren't you going to invite me in?" The big smile I have on my face is beginning to tremble away.

"Sure, honey. I'm sorry, I'm just real surprised to see you out in this storm." He looks down at the overnight bag in my hand and takes it from me. He urges me inside and closes the door to shield us from the storm behind me.

"I need to tell you something," Hart voice trails off as a striking woman walks down his stairs in nothing but a man's shirt…his shirt.

I look over at Hart with a surprised look on my face. Then, I look back at the stairs where the woman has paused in mid-step.

"Hart, wha…what's going on?" I stutter out.

I take in a deep breath, trying my best to remain calm and rational without jumping into any conclusion too fast.

"Well?" I cross my arms as I glare at him. I'm trying my best to control the look of accusation I'm bestowing on him but it's not happening.

"Who is this?" The woman has come more into my view and I recognize her as the woman from the restaurant almost a month ago. She saunters down the stairs to stand at Hart's—my Hart's—side as if she has every right to be there.

"Not now, Sabrina," Hart says without taking his troubled eyes off of me. "Can you go back upstairs and put your clothes on? Why are you in my shirt anyway?" He turns and looks at her with a frown on his face.

"Out of your closet, silly. Where do you think?" She trails her long, French manicured nails up his muscular arm. I cringe at the sight of her touching him so boldly.

"Did I interrupt something? Because…"

"No, Whitney. You didn't interrupt anything."

"Speak for yourself, Hart. I need you and you promised to be here for me. She needs to go." She looks at me with a sneer to her thin lips as if she smells something unsavory. Then, she looks towards him as tears suddenly pop in her eyes. She starts to bawl like a baby on cue.

"Don't cry, Sabrina, your dad will be okay," he says, allowing her to fall into his open arms. And just like that, he seems to forget about me as he comforts his ex-girlfriend. Or is she even his ex?

"Damn you, Hart," I shout out, feeling disillusioned.

I press the back of my hand to my mouth to cut off lashing ugly words at him. I straighten my spine and arch my shoulders. Maybe I should just give up and walk away. The wall is there for me to see. The writing has formed in perfect bold print. No fancy cursive or unbroken lines. Just plain and to the point. I exhale the stale breath that seems to be trapped in my lungs for the longest time. I revert into my shell and walk over to my overnight bag to pick it up.

I take one step, two steps, towards the front door, when Hart's deep, ragged voice stops me into my third step. I look over my right shoulder and he untangles himself from Sabrina's clutches.

A single tear runs down my cheek and leaves behind a glistening trail of my pain. I stand still as a statue as Hart walks slowly towards me on booted feet. The closer he gets to me, the shell around my heart is shattering away…piece by piece.

"You don't have to leave. I can explain. Will you please wait upstairs in my bedroom?"

I'm so torn between going and staying. Honestly, I don't even know what to do. *What should I do? What would you do?* I question myself, over and over.

"Let her go, Hart," Sabrina says behind me. "I need you," she pleads.

In that moment, something rebels inside me. I decide to do the opposite of what I would've done on previous occasions. Instead of running, I make up my mind to stay. I bite my bottom lip to quell my emotions and find my voice to speak. "I'll stay," I reply, looking into his eyes. In that moment, it's just me and Hart in the room.

"Good, thank you. You've made the right decision, trusting me. I'll be up in a few minutes. I promise," he adds as he looks into my troubled eyes.

I walk up the stairs without another word, ignoring the fiery look of dissatisfaction that Sabrina has in her eyes. I'm not sure that I trust him completely but I will hear him out.

I stand in his room peering out the window at the turbulent night. After a short while, I let the drapery fall as I turn away from the window and walk over to sit on the edge of Hart's bed. The same bed he made love to me in. The bedroom door opens and closes as Hart walks over to the bed to stare down at me.

"Are you okay?" he asks.

"I don't know. It all depends on what you're about to tell me as to why your ex-girlfriend is here in your house, walking down the stairs in nothing but your shirt?"

"She's in my house because a taxi dropped her off here and I let her in. She was upset because her dad was in a car wreck and she had been at the hospital all day with him and her mother. She didn't have anyone else to talk to."

"That doesn't explain why she was in your shirt when I got here." I jumped off the bed and gave him an accusing stare.

"I don't know what Sabrina was thinking. She asked to use the bathroom. Then, when you showed up, she came down the stairs in my shirt. I promise you there is nothing more to that, Whitney. I have straightened her out about taking off her clothes and I will never fall for her sob stories again. I do care for her as a friend, but not if it will come between us. She and I have no romantic involvement and, after the things I just told her, she's clear on that."

I search his eyes to see if I can detect any sign of lying. If he's lying, he's good at it. All I can see is the truth lurking in their depths. "Where is she now?"

"I called a taxi for her. I wanted to comfort her during this trying time for her, but I couldn't allow her to stay here and cause trouble for us. My loyalty lies with you."

"If I wouldn't have shown up here tonight, would you have let her stay?"

"Sure, I would've let her stay long enough to help her in any way I could and then sent her on her way," he admits with sincerity.

"But what if she would've come downstairs in that T-shirt and I wasn't here?"

"Then, she would've been sent on her way much sooner with the same choice words I gave her before I sent her home tonight. I don't appreciate that stunt any more than you do."

"Good, because I won't play second fiddle to anyone. The last thing I intend to do is intrude in a place where I'm not wanted."

"How can you doubt that you're wanted? You are very much wanted here," he says and stretches his arms wide as if to encompass his home. "And here," he touches a space in his heart. "Don't you realize how much I love you and how much I've always loved you, Whitney Martin?"

I look down at the floor, trying to give myself time to take all of this in. His finger lifts my chin so he can peer into my eyes.

"I love you too Hart," I say. "I'm sorry that I didn't realize your love for me back then. But I'm glad that we found our way to each other. Because I truly do love you." I feel so vulnerable as I admit my true feelings. Hart has a way of making me let go.

"I want to make love to you, Whitney. I want to hold you in my arms all night long. Please tell me you want the same thing," he begs.

"Hart, I do want to make love with you too," I barely get out my reply before he hauls me into his embrace and kisses me senseless. His tongue flicks in and out of my mouth as he plays cat and mouse with me. A piercing throb invades my inner walls as his arousal pokes me in my belly.

"You smell so good," his lips trail to the side of my face and neckline as he takes the time to inhale my scent. His hands are like an octopus as they begin touching my face, my shoulders, arms and breasts.

His hand wanders back down as he kisses me again. Eventually, his hand skims over my soft belly area before lifting the edge of my shirt to get to my braless breast.

"No bra," he mummers against my lips before thrusting his tongue deeply into my mouth.

"No bra," I agree as his hand cups my breast and his thumb flicks back and forth across my nipple. "Ahhhh," sounds of ecstasy escapes my lips.

He removes my clothes piece by piece, until I'm standing before him completely nude. "You're overdressed now," I look at him through lust-glazed eyes.

"Not for long, sweetheart," he promises as he kicks off his boots and I help him divest of his shirt, jeans and underwear, all in record time. "I'm starving for your pussy," he tells me just before pushing me back onto the bed and sets his course of planting kisses over my entire body. His hot tongue licks at my nipples, before dropping tender kisses all over my belly. He moves down, dropping more kisses on my pelvic then pubic bone. I moan aloud, when he drapes my thighs over his shoulders and dives in like a man on a mission.

Finally, I think as my pussy throbs and feeds him my nectar. His tongue swipes my entire pubic area from front to back. Wetness seeps down my thighs as he pays special attention to my throbbing clitoris.

Hart goes from gently kissing and nibbling his way around and inside my slick folds to thrusting inside my core with his thick tongue. My hips lift and I grind myself onto his mouth for all that I'm worth. "Ooh, Hart, baby, what are you doing?" I cry out.

He answers me by spreading my labia apart and sucking on each of my inner lips before switching to kissing and licking my outer lips. I should probably be furious right now, but that tongue of his is driving me insane as I thrash beneath him like a woman starving for more. I weep into his mouth an earth shattering orgasm. His lapping sounds are loud as he swallows my essence with relish.

I tremble when he slides up my body and hovers over me on his elbows. He then takes one warm hand to push my thighs further apart. His desire-filled eyes burn into mine. "You're mine," he grates thrusting his nine-inch erection into my pulsating walls. His thrusts aren't as gentle as the last time we made love, but I don't want them to be. This is what my body has been yearning for. Hart embedded deep within me with no mercy. "No one will come between us," he adds on a grunt.

I wrap my legs around his trim waist as his pumps grow bolder and bolder. My lusty cries grow louder and louder and his animalistic grunts turn me on so much that I ricochet into a massive explosion. My walls go into a convulsive state and squeeze the life out of his big cock.

"Arrgh shit, I'm fucking cumming," he hisses out as his seed spits out inside my core. Completely satiated, he rolls off of me and pulls me close to his side.

"Explosive," he says and place a kiss on top of my head.

"Yes, explosive," I agree drowsily and fall right to sleep in his strong arms.

*

Despite the early hour of the morning, I lay in delightful splendor. I know I shouldn't be this deliriously happy, but I am. There's both a thrum of excitement that courses through my body and a hint of anxiety that makes me wonder if this is too good to be true. I yawn and reach over for Hart but I encounter nothing but empty space.

How long has he been up, I wonder? I look over at his bedside clock and note it's a little before seven o'clock. Suddenly, I can smell the scent of fresh-brewed coffee in the air and know that he's in the kitchen. It has to be a strong brew for the aroma to waft upstairs in this huge home.

I jump out of the bed and grab my overnight bag that Hart has already placed at the foot of the bed. I walk into his adjoining bathroom, take a shower and brush my teeth, before getting dressed and heading down the stairs.

I pause just outside of the kitchen door to listen as Hart's sings along with the radio. I smile at the sound of his deep and sensual voice. The sound makes me happy to hear it first thing in the morning. I push the door open and walk inside. I can see that Hart is also already dressed for the day.

"Good morning, my love," Hart says, upon hearing me enter the kitchen.

“Good morning, honey,” I walk up behind him to wrap my arms around his waist and press my face against his back. I close my eyes to inhale his fresh and clean scent as he flips pancakes on a griddle.

He stops what he is doing for a second and places a soft kiss onto my lips. "Please, have a seat and I'll get you a cup of coffee, after I plate our pancakes." "Unless you prefer something else," he adds.

"Coffee sounds wonderful," I say. "But you don't have to wait on me like that. Just point me to the cups and I'll get my own," I add.

"Nonsense, I won't have it. I want to wait on you, so sit down and relax, please."

I walk over to the table and take a seat as he asks. I'm so not used to any man I've ever dated waiting on me like this. I went to sleep last night smiling and I wake up smiling. A woman can really get used to this.

"Sweetheart, I want you to eat up. Breakfast is the most important meal for champions," he says as he places a nice plate of bacon, pancakes and eggs on the table in front of me.

"Thank you," I say as he sits down across from me with his own plate.

"You're welcome, baby. I hope you slept well last night," he says with a teasing glint in his eyes.

"I slept too good," I reply and dig into my food with gusto after he blesses the food. "You can really cook. This is so good," I tell him.

"My parent's housekeeper Mattie taught me how to cook before I went away for college."

"Wow, you had a housekeeper?" I stop eating enough to look at him across the table.

"Yes, but just because I grew up privileged, I just want you to know that I have never taken advantage of my blessings in life or thought I was better than anyone else, no matter their position in life."

"You don't have to explain. I already know you're humble and you aren't a snob. You never have been."

"I'm glad you know that. Because my parents have a house on Martha's Vineyard and they want me to bring my girlfriend. I want you to come with me," he says before taking a sip from his coffee cup.

"Do they know you broke up with Sabrina?"

"Yes."

"Did you tell your parents about me, or about who I am, or anything like that?" I ask him. I think he knows that I'm trying to avoid asking the obvious question.

"I just told them that I met the love of my life and that Sabrina and I didn't work out."

"But, I think you should—"

"Look at the time," he cuts me off getting up. "We better hurry if we don't want to be late for work. You know how morning traffic can get."

"You're right." I let my concerns go about meeting his parents. Glancing at the clock, I jump up and help him clear the table. "I'll see you later," I say once we make it out of the house. I encircle his neck to give him a goodbye kiss before getting in my car.

"I'll miss you. Will you go with me to meet my parents?"

I bite my bottom lip. "Yes. How long will we be staying?"

"Just the weekend. I'll use my company helicopter to fly us out."

"You know how to fly a helicopter?"

"Of course I do. Don't look so worried. You couldn't be in safer hands," he says, closing my car door.

"Okay, if you say so," I reply before starting my ignition. I blow him a quick kiss and drive around the circular driveway before easing onto the roadway.

Chapter 15

HART

"Hart, thank you for coming with me to meet my mother," she tells me as I pull up in her mother's gravel driveway.

"You're welcome, sweetheart. It's only fair that I meet your mother, especially since you've agreed to meet mine."

"True," she says as I open the car door for her to get out. We walk up to the Beech Wood ranch style home. I look around, admiring it all.

"Did you grow up in this house?" I ask her as she rings her mother's doorbell.

"I sure did. My bedroom is still the same as it was when I left for college," she says with a giggle.

"Whit, I'm happy to see you made it," a woman who is the spitting image of Whitney opens the door. I'm glad you brought your young man with you too," she gives me the once over as she steps back to allow us inside.

"Thank you, Mrs. Martin. I appreciate you for inviting me here. You have such a lovely home, by the way."

"Thank you, Hart, right?"

"Yes ma'am, Hart Strong at your service," I say with a smile.

"Whit, I like this young man already."

"I love him too, mother," Whitney admits. Her mother's eyes widen in surprise by her daughter's admission of love. Whitney turns, looks at me and smiles.

"Alright then. Since Hart likes my home, you may show him around while I put the meal on the table. And be sure the two of you wash your hands before coming to my table," she directs.

"Yes mother," Whitney says as she places a kiss on her mother's cheek. "Come on." Whitney takes my hand and shows me through the one-level home with three bedrooms, two baths, and a family room where a large, flat screen television hangs from the wall.

"I especially love your bedroom. I didn't know you were into collecting stuffed animals. Had I known, I would've gotten you some."

"I used to be into collecting all kinds of stuffed animals. I outgrew it after a while, but I didn't have the heart to get rid of them. So, I just left them in my old bedroom. That way, I can revisit old memories from time to time. My dad bought the majority of those for me," I admit, feeling a mist of tears enter my eyes.

"You still miss your dad. It must be hard for you and your mother not to have him around, especially during the holidays." I pull Whitney's head to my chest and hug her close to me.

"Yes, it is. The thing is, he was so much into the holidays when I was growing up. Even after I went away to college and came back home during the winter break, he would have the outside of the house lit up and the inside was decorated as well. He was so into the holiday spirit. We still kept the family tradition of driving out to Huckleberry Tree Farm every year to pick out the biggest and tallest Christmas tree. Mother used to say, 'Charles, there's no way in hell we're getting that tree through the front door'. But dad, always said, 'You just wait and see. This tree will make it inside the front door, come hell or high water'," she laughs at the memory. "But, guess what?"

"He could never get it through the front door, right?" I guess.

"Right," she replies and we laugh together. "He would always have to get the saw and trim it down. And mother would say, 'I told you so Charles. When are you ever going to listen to reason?' He would just turn to her and take her in his arms and kiss her until she forgot about what she told him."

"Seems like your dad was a good man. I wish I could have met him to thank him personally for being a part of bringing you into this world. Because you, my love, are the perfect fit for me. I'm sure he had a lot to do with molding you into the woman you are today."

"Thanks Hart. That means a lot to me," she says and swipes away another tear that's threatening to fall.

I steal a quick kiss from her tempting lips, just before she leads me into the kitchen. The open-concept kitchen is in close proximity to the dining room. It's full of delightful smells of onions, peppers and other pleasant spices that set off a cheery vibe.

"Dinner is ready," Mrs. Martin announces. "I hope you both brought your appetites."

"Wow, I definitely brought my appetite," I say looking at the plated dishes of baked Cornish hens, dirty rice, and asparagus. We have glasses of ice cold sweet tea to drink. I seat Whitney's mother first and then Whitney, before taking a seat myself.

"Hart, if you don't mind, will you do me the honors of blessing our meal?" Mrs. Martin asks.

"It will be my pleasure," I reply. We join hands as I proceed to bless our food. "Heavenly Father, thank you for the blessings of the two magnificent ladies around this table. Thank you, for the invitation into this lovely home and thank you for the hands that prepared this scrumptious looking feast. May this food be blessed with plentiful nourishments for our temples. Continue to keep us all in your arms eternally, now and forever. Amen."

Mrs. Martin gives Whitney an approving eye before saying, "Thanks so much for that spirit-led prayer. I felt that young man."

"You're welcome," I say, not knowing where the words came from. I'm far from a saint, but I was raised to be a praying man.

Between bites of the delicious food, Whitney's mother asks me questions to try to get to know me better. I don't mind her questions at all. I expect nothing less of a mother looking out for her child.

"Whitney tells me you're in the construction business. How is that working out for you?"

"Business is doing very well and I expect it to continue doing so in the unforeseeable future. I think my company has built a solid reputation to stand behind the work we do."

I look over at Whitney and give her a quick wink. A blush rises to her cheeks as she sends me a smile that lights up her beautiful eyes.

"That's great. I'm really glad to hear it. So many businesses have been going under. I'm also proud of my daughter. She is doing big things in her business as well…Sierra as well," she adds.

"I'm very proud of Whitney too. She works very hard and deserves all sorts of rewards," I reply and reach under the table to slide my hand under Whitney's skirt and squeeze her supple thigh.

I send her a wicked glance and she starts to cough as her bite of food goes down the wrong pipe. "Are you alright?" both me and her mother ask at the same time.

"Yes." She picks up her glass and takes a long swallow. I smirk and she glares at me. I have a hard time holding in my laughter.

"So, Whitney tells me that you'll be taking her to meet your parents next weekend in Martha's Vineyard," her mother speaks, directing my attention back towards her.

"Yes, ma'am," I reply and take a sip of my ice tea.

"I'm really looking forward in meeting them," Whitney joins in.

"Do your parents' realize you're dating a black woman?" her mother asks bluntly.

"Mother," Whitney start to say, but her mother cuts in.

"Pardon me if my questions seem intrusive, but you are my only daughter and I, as your mother, am within my rights. And before you even go there, I know you're a grown woman and all but you're still my child. You'll still be my child when I'm old and gray and you have to mash up my food in order for me to eat."

I begin laughing and can't stop. Whitney gives me a look that says, 'I don't see anything funny,' so I rein my laughter in. "I'm sorry," I mutter with repentance. "But to answer your question, no, I haven't told my parents that Whitney is black. Whitney's color is irrelevant. The only thing that matters is that she's the woman I love and will one day make my wife," I simply state.

Whitney gasps and her fork clatters loudly against her plate as she drops it. "Oh, I had no idea that you and my daughter were that serious. But I should have known better once she informed me that you wanted to take her to meet your parents. It's all good and well that you think there will be no turbulence with your parents accepting my daughter. I hope that you are correct in your assumptions. If the situation takes a turn for the worse, I want to make myself plain and clear when I say this. I don't want my daughter hurt or abused in any shape or form. You and your parents will have me to deal with if that happens, which I pray it doesn't."

I give Mrs. Martin a look of respect and glance over at Whitney and her mouth is still open in surprise as she visibly winces from her mother's blunt words. I reach over, grasp her hand, bring it to my lips and place a kiss on it. I look back over to Mrs. Martin.

"I'm very serious about your daughter. I will never allow anyone hurt her, while she is in and out of my care. I will protect her with my life if it comes down to it. I love her just that much, ever since I was a teenager. I loved your daughter when she didn't even remember I existed. Now that she knows I exist and is ready to accept my love, I'm never letting her go. Not for anyone."

"Oh, my," Mrs. Martin touches her heart and tears appear in her eyes. Eyes that are so much like her daughter's. "All I have to say on that is welcome to the family, son." She gives me a warm smile, which is the replica of Whitney's.

"Thank you, mom, I accept," I say, winning her over. I give her a charming smile. Deep down, I'm just hoping the meeting goes as well with my parents. Because the Strong's can sometimes be unpredictable as I know all too well.

Chapter 16

WHITNEY

I walk into W & S design a little later than I normally would since I overslept in Hart's arms this morning. Both of us seem to be doing a lot of that over the past few days.

"Good morning, Paula," I say in a sing-song voice as I pass by the receptionist desk. "I stopped off at Starbucks and got us a Frappuccino and a pastry." I sit her bag on the desk.

"Good morning, Whitney, and thanks so much for the breakfast," she returns with a friendly smile. "You must know that I skipped breakfast this morning and I'm in dire need of this pick me up." She grins as if the contents of her cup are a piece of heaven.

"Good, it's right on time then." I flash her a smile and continue to walk down the hallway into the office to see Sierra bent over the printer. "Good morning, my dear," I call out to her and place her drink and pastry on her desk. "I brought us breakfast."

"Good morning and thanks," she replies with a tremble in her voice as if she's been crying. She continues looking down with her hair shielding her face.

"What's wrong, Sierra? And I don't want to hear "nothing" this time."

She cuts off the printer and turns to face me. Her eyes are red rimmed and puffy from crying. I hurriedly put down my belongings and rush over to her side.

"The weekend that I went home." She sniffs as she tries to get her words out.

"Go on," I say, encouraging her. I can tell she's battling with holding her tears in.

"I…I," she attempts again to get her words out but fails miserably. Her pain seems to be too much for her to take as beads of water start to fall from her eyes and down to her cheeks, one after another.

I grasp her in an embrace and she clings to me as if she's holding on for dear life. Heart wrenching sobs escape through her body and muffle themselves against my chest, as I try to comfort her. But from what, I don't know. So, I just continue to allow her to cry out her tears and I hold her until her tears are spent.

"Okay, let's try this again," I say, leading her over to a small couch in the corner of the office. I sit beside her and look into her eyes. I reach for a couple of Kleenexes from a nearby table to give her. She blows her nose noisily before she begins to speak.

"I found a lump in my breast. I had a mammogram last week and I should get the results back sometime today. The diagnostic center will call me. If the results are good, I'll get them over the phone, but if not I'll have to go in for a biopsy. I'm so scared," she says as tears begin to fall again.

"Please, don't panic," I try to calm her. "You are young and your lump may be related to your menstrual cycle. At least that's what the doctor told me when I was going through this with my mother. Of course, you'll have to get your results to be sure. How about you do this...Calm down and try not to stress over it until the results of your mammogram are in." I say this although I'm a mess inside thinking of the unthinkable. I can't allow her to see me fall apart though. I must keep up a strong appearance and be a voice of stability for her sake.

"That's easy for you to say. You're not the one who found a lump in your breast."

"You're right. But one thing I learned when my own mother went through her health scare two years ago is that stressing only does more damage in the end."

"I'm so sorry, Whit. In my worrying about myself, I forgot your mother went through the same thing."

"Don't worry about it, honey. Believe me, I understand. I just don't want you to make yourself sick worrying about it. I'm here for you and if I have to cancel my trip tomorrow to the Hampton's with Hart that's just what I'm going to do."

"I won't let you," Sierra bristles at my statement. "There's no way I'm letting you get out of meeting your man's parents. Don't you dare think about it."

"It's no biggie," I reply, biting my bottom lip.

"Look at you, you're just as scared to meet Hart's parents as I am about finding out my mammogram results. Don't use me as an excuse to get out of meeting them. You either meet them now or later. My advice to you is to bite the bullet and get it over with."

"You're right," I reply.

"I'm going to tell you what you just told me…don't stress about it. Stress only bring on more problems."

"You're right again," I say with a laugh. "Go drink your Frappuccino, before it turns cold."

"Did you bring me my favorite raspberry pastry?" Sierra asks me as she is walking towards her desk.

"You know it," I said, standing and walking towards my own desk to get as much work out the way as possible, so I can have my weekend relatively free.

"Oh, goody." She smiles for the first time since I arrived. I watch her remove the pastry from the bag and take a big bite. She closes her eyes and makes a pleasurable moan. "This is better than sex, not that I'm getting any." She laughs and I join in.

My workday passes by faster than usual and lunch hour is upon us before we know it. The telephone rings and Sierra answers it. "Hello, yes, put him through please," she says looking over at me and covers the mouthpiece of the phone. "It's AUD diagnostics," she whispers with a look of concern in her eyes.

My stomach muscles spasm and tighten. I place my hands on my lap and whisper a silent prayer that she will hear good news. I also cross my fingers for good measure.

"I see," Sierra says.

Her one-sided conversation makes me nervous. I have to force myself not to pick up the phone and listen to her conversation from my extension.

"Thank you soooo much," Sierra says and a big smile stretches across her lips. Her eyes light with happiness as she looks across the room at me. She shoots me a thumb up sign and I finally let out a sigh of relief. "Goodbye," she says, ending the call.

We both jump up from our seats and run into each other arms. "Thank you, God!" I shout out. "I told you everything would work out."

"Yes you did," she replies. "And since you treated me to breakfast…I'm treating you to lunch. Get your purse and let's go."

"Where are we going?"

"To Taqueria del Sol," she replies.

"Yes…you don't have to ask me twice," I reply walking over to remove my purse from my bottom desk drawer.

I can already taste their famous shrimp chowder on my tongue and, if it wasn't a damn shame to be drunk at work, I would enjoy a margarita right along with it. We head out the office door pumped and ready to have an alcohol-free celebration of Sierra's diagnostic test being negative.

Chapter 17

HART

"Are you comfortable, baby?" I ask a tight-faced Whitney as she grips the helicopter seat with her French tipped nails.

"Uh-huh," she gives a quick jerky nod of her head. She tells me otherwise but I know she's half frightened to death.

"Try to relax, sweetheart. It won't take no more than an hour and a half to reach the Hamptons. I'm an experienced pilot and have over fourteen thousand hours of experience."

"I'm fine," she says this while nibbling at her bottom lip.

"Okay, I'll have to take your word for it. You'll need to wear these," I say, helping her slide on a pair of headphones to help protect her ears from the loud helicopter. "You can speak to me through here," I adjust the small microphone close to her lips. She nods her head as I adjust the other headphones over my ears and start up the D500 four-door, five-seat copter.

The wop, wop sound from the turning blades of the helicopter is blaring. I give all of my attention to flying, since I need both my hands and feet.

“That wasn’t too bad,” Whitney speaks up an hour and a half later as I maneuver the helicopter to hover towards a private landing on a slope. She cocks her head in my direction. I can feel her eyes studying me as I operate the controls.

“I told you,” I reply as I take great care to place the tail rotor in a position where it will strike the ground. I glance her way, and she raises her chin to meet my eyes. My chest begins to rise and fall with rapid breaths. “You take my breath away,” I say, before returning my attention to landing.

She places a hand on my thigh. “You are everything I’ve ever wanted in a man and more.”

Naturally, a smile curves around my lips at her revelation. I can’t wait to get her alone, so that I can have my way with her once again. I take off my seatbelt and earphones. I then assist Whitney with her seatbelt as she takes off her earphones and lays them aside. Our eyes meet and she licks her plump lips. I inhale sharply as the sexual tension sizzles between us like slow burning embers before catching into flame. It appears that flying high has hurled both us into a passionate spiral.

"The ride home will be so much better," I tell her, breaking the spell. I open my door and hop down to the ground. I trot around and open her door, wrapping my hands around her waist to help her out.

"My legs are wobbly." She laughs and holds on to my forearms for balance. She purses her lips and I can't resist their sweetness as they lure me to do what I've wanted to do the entire ride here.

"Maybe this'll make it better." My head swoops down to assault her lips with my own. At the very first touch of my lips, her eyes close and mine soon follow suit. I bring my right hand up to caress her right cheek and urge her to open her mouth to receive the exploration of my tongue. Her mouth opens beneath mine to allow my tongue inside to partake in her sweetness as our kiss deepens.

"Ahem," someone clears their throat, trying to get our attention.

I reluctantly pull away from my tempting lady to see who is intruding on our private moment. "Henry," I say to the driver, who I had forgot was meeting us at the landing strip to take us to my family's private vacation home.

"Good to see you again Hart," Henry greets me.

"Good to see you too." I step forward to shake his hand and clasp him firmly on his shoulder. "Whitney," I say looking back at her and she immediately steps to my side. "Henry Davis, this is my girlfriend, Whitney Martin."

"Nice to meet you, young lady," Henry eyes crinkle at the corners as he looks from me to Whitney in surprise. His teeth gleam white against his dark, mahogany skin tone.

"It's good to meet you too," Mr. Davis."

"You can call me Henry…just like Hart does," he replies.

"Only if you will call me Whitney or Whit for short," she says.

"I've never been one for messing up a beautiful name by shortening it, so Whitney it is," Henry replies with a chuckle. "The car awaits," he adds as he helps me remove the bags from the helicopter's storage area to the black Rolls-Royce Phantom EWB.

"Hart, just to give you a heads up. Your parents are planning some sort of fancy party tomorrow night," he says as he drives towards the big Victorian style home on the coastal beach. From the outside, I appreciate the noncontemporary style and elegance of the beachfront houses and remember the fun times I had coming here during the summer as a teenager.

"Thank you for the warning, Henry." I glance sideways at Whitney. She remains silent and is peering straight ahead at the big white house that looms up the winding long driveway.

"We're here," I say to Whitney as if she doesn't see the obvious when the car comes to a stop in front of my parents' large home.

"I see," she replies.

Henry walks around to open the door. Whitney slides out and I follow.

I place a comforting hand at the small of her back. "I'll take the heaviest bag, Henry," I say as I pick up Whitney's bag and lead her towards the front door. Henry is close behind us.

"The air even smells different here and the ocean looks magnificent from here," Whitney says.

"Yes, I think so too. On top of that, the beach and this entire neighborhood is very private and quiet."

"Are you telling me that your family owns their own private beach?" she asks.

"Yes. Hopefully we can make use of it before we leave," I whisper seductively in her ear. In that moment, Rosie, the head housekeeper opens the front door.

"Hart," she says and opens her arms to me.

"Hello Rosie," I step away from Whitney to embrace Rosie. She has also been with my family for at least fourteen years.

"Who do you have with you?" Rosie eyes Whitney with curiosity.

"This is Whitney Martin. The love of my life," I reply.

"Oh, my, is this the same girl you use to tell me about during the summers you came here as a teenager?

"She's one and the same." I look down at Whitney and she has a bewildered expression on her face.

"Welcome, Miss Martin," Rosie turns toward Whitney with a friendly smile planted on her lips. Her aquamarine eyes twinkle.

"I can't believe you talked about me like that," Whitney steps in closer to me and whispers as a blush infuses beneath her cheeks. "Nice to meet you, Miss Rosie," Whitney says in a louder voice.

"It's a real pleasure meeting you, Miss Martin," Rosie's eyes crease at the corner as she steps aside for us to enter.

"Wow." Whitney's eyebrows arch and her mouth gapes opens wide the moment we step through the front door of the spacious foyer.

"You like?"

"I love what I've seen so far and I'm sure I'll like the rest."

"Wait until you see the twenty-two hundred square foot covered porch. I want you to see both the sunrise and sunset out there. I don't know which is more beautiful, although they both are spectacular," I add.

"Your parents' are in the parlor," Rosie says.

"I'll see them a little later. I want to show Whitney to our room. I'll take it from here," I tell both Rosie and Henry. "I'm sure you both have more important things to do than to be bothered with me."

"You are never a bother, Hart. You've always been low maintenance. You never wanted anyone to wait on you hand and foot," says Rosie.

"Indeed," Henry says and hands over the bags to me. Whitney picks up the smaller one. "He always has been an independent boy. You have a keeper here," Henry adds, before I walk Whitney up the stairs to my bedroom. I don't care how it looks, I want Whitney there.

"This is it," I say to Whitney once we enter my bedroom that has dark-colored blue accent walls and beautiful painted murals on the wall. There's hardwood flooring, with a large, scattered rug gracing the floor. There is a custom made bed directly in the center of the room with accent pillows and two side tables placed on each side of the bed.

"I can't believe that you have a jukebox," she toys with a curly lock of her hair.

"Yeah." I sit our bags down and look over at the jukebox sitting in the corner of the room. "It belonged to my grandfather. I had it restored a while ago and felt its rightful place was here, where I had so many great times with him."

"This house belonged to him?" She looks up at me with curiosity.

"Yes, it did. He and my grandmother had many happy years here." I scratch the side of my close-cropped beard as I reflect inwardly on my grandparents. "The bathroom is through there if you need to use it."

We head down to the parlor to meet my parents. Whitney looks nervous and I anxiously reach for her hand to capture in my own. Marylyn and Hartland Strong Sr.'s conversation ceases as their eyes beam on the two of us standing in the parlor doorway. Maybe, I shouldn't have led Whitney into this meeting with my parent's blindly. But this is the only recourse. I didn't want to give either my parents or Whitney any room for backing out of this meeting.

"Hartland," my father's voice booms out as he stands to his full height. My mother stands beside him and a lackluster smile forms on her lips. I cringe at the full use of my name. I have always gone by the name Hart, even for business purposes, and he knows this.

"Father and mother, I want you to meet my girlfriend, Whitney Martin," I say, looping my arm around her waist to pull her closer to my side. I can feel a tremble go through her body so I give her a firm squeeze for encouragement.

"But what is the meaning of this, Hartland?"

Yikes, my mother never calls me Hartland.

"What do you mean, mother?" I amble over to stand before my parents with Whitney by my side. I release her briefly to embrace my mother and place a kiss against her cheek. "Father." I lean over to give him a hearty one-armed embrace.

"Did you just say this is your girlfriend, son?" Both are my parents are giving Whitney and me a hard stare.

"It's so nice to meet you, Mr. and Mrs. Strong. You two have a very lovely home."

"Thank you dear," my mother replies and my father indicates we should have a seat.

"Forgive us, Miss Martin, is it?" My father's brow arches haughtily.

"Yes sir," Whitney answers, while fiddling with the small locket around her neck. "But you may call me Whitney." A shy smile forms on her lips.

"Very well...Whitney, it is. Forgive our surprise at seeing you with our son. He didn't inform us that..."

"Well, dear, what Hartland is trying to say is that he didn't expect a woman of color to be dating our son. I don't mean any disrespect, mind you."

I send a worried glance Whitney's way. She sits beside me slack mouthed. She tries to viciously yank her hand from mine but I tighten my hold. Her body stiffens and I know that I have to do something…to say something to quell the tension that's swirling in the atmosphere.

"Mother, I really don't think that's appropriate," I call her out on her callus behavior. "I love Whitney and I expect you and father to treat her with the utmost respect while she is under the Strong's household. I have never, ever, disrespected either of you as my parents. But I will not allow either of you to hurt the woman that I hope to one day be my wife and the mother of my kids…Your grandchildren," I narrow my eyes at the both of them.

My father's face turns crimson with fury. His lips grow into a straight line. His mouth opens and closes, before my mother reaches over to touch his hand. A look passes between them, before they direct their attention to the two of us. Mother suddenly smiles, concealing the agitated look that was in her blue eyes just moments before.

“I've brought tea." Rosie rolls in a tea trolley, cutting off the rest of my words. On the tea tray Rosie rolls in are bite-sized sandwiches and decadent looking buttery scones on a tiered tray as well. “I figure Hart and his lady can use a tad bit of refreshment to hold them over until dinnertime.”

"Right on time, Rosie. You really do have the most impeccable timing," Mother is the first one to speak.

"Thank you, ma'am. How do you want your tea?" Rosie asks Whitney.

"Two cubes of sugar please but no milk."

Rosie pours the tea up into a delicate china cup and drops two sugar cubes before passing over the teacup and saucer to Whitney.

“Thank you, Rosie,” Whitney says and gives her a friendly smile.

“You’re very welcome, miss.” Rosie begins to pour the rest of our tea and passes them around as well.

“I need to have words with you later,” Whitney whispers to me as I pass her a sandwich from the small tray. I quickly look at her and can see anger sizzling in the depths of her brown eyes.

I draw in a sharp breath and eagerly bite into my sandwich to ward off the tongue lashing I know I'm in for. Without a doubt, I deserve every angry word she throws at me. As long as she doesn't leave me, I'm good. Her leaving me won't be an option, whether my parents accept her or not will be their decision, but whether I will allow her to walk out of my life, rests entirely with me.

Chapter 18

WHITNEY

I hope that I don't regret Hart talking me into staying here. The talk I had with him the day before seemed to comfort me on some level. He assured me that things would get better if I just stuck it out. One weekend won't be too much to do, I decide. One dinner party, that's all. I breathe in and exhale to calm my nerves but there is a knot in the pit of my stomach that won't go away.

Midway through my second glass of wine I realize that I need something more substantial to eat or I'm going to have a horrible hangover in the morning. I don't need to be nursing a sore head or a queasy stomach because Hart's parents are enough trouble to give me all three.

"Dinner is served," the announcement is made by a different maid that I haven't seen since getting here the day before. I'm relieved that I'm about to put something on my stomach. However, my night takes a turn for the worse the moment Hart's ex-girlfriend, Sabrina Woods, walks through the door. Had I known earlier that she'd be here, I would have not come. I begin to drink wine like it is water. My nerves are literally shot at the sight of her.

I turn up my wine glass to drain the rest of its fruity contents as I look between Sabrina and Hart. She's dressed in an artistic, short, black dress that clings to her every perfect little curve. Her dress is sleeveless, revealing toned tanned arms that will rival Michelle Obama's. She immediately begins to sink her hooks into Hart after she arrives and, by the looks of it, she's winning. She can't seem to keep her hands off of him and she's flirting with him every chance she gets. What's worse is he's laughing and smiling with her and the other guests as if everything is honky dory.

I look up at the ceiling and wonder how am I going to make it through this dinner. I can feel my belly rumbling just as I follow the rest of the guests into the dining room and sit down at the elegantly dressed table. My name plate is arranged across the table from my boyfriend and his ex. Hart finally looks over at me. *Oh, he finally remembered I was in the room*, I think as I glare at him with disappointment. As tempting as it is to tuck my tail between my legs and run, my hunger is winning at the moment.

How in the hell am I sitting across from Hart and Sabrina is sitting right next to him? Is he the type of man that lets his parents run his life? The type to let Sabrina play him like a fined tuned piano?

After this fine meal, I'll tell him and his snooty parents what I think of them. I don't care who likes it either. Every last one of them can go to hell with gasoline drawers on for all I care.

"Yippy, more wine," I mutter as the server in all black pours wine into our glasses. I look up at the brilliant beauty of the chandelier before picking up my glass and raising it in the air. I glare at Hart as I lift my glass. In my mind, it's my farewell drink—an ode to what I thought we had. His eyes soften as he looks at me but mine harden as I tilt my wine glass to my lips and drain its contents once again. I'm not a drinker at all, so dinner passes in a blur.

"Let's all move into the drawing room, shall we?" Mr. Strong asks.

I sit up straight from my wilting position at the dining room table. I reach for my glass of wine and bring it to my lips, but the glass is empty. "I think you've had enough for one night," Hart's breath brushes against my ear.

"Where did you come from?" I slur my words. I try to stand, but my legs lazily betray me as I slump back down onto my seat. "Why aren't you with your girlfriend?" My tongue feels thick in my mouth as I form the words.

"You're my girlfriend, Whitney," he replies and half lifts me as he pulls me to his side.

"Are you coming Hart?" I look up and Sabrina is staring daggers my way from her stony blue eyes. "Aha, looks like someone can't hold their liquor," her eyes gleam with deviltry and she bares her fangs in a trill laugh. I can feel curious eyes on me as Hart helps me to my feet. I suddenly feel dizzy and grudgingly lean against Hart for support.

"You know what?" I say, glaring at all the lily white faces looking at me as if I don't belong.

"Don't Whitney," Hart tries to quiet me.

"Shush…" I place one finger against his lips. "I've been quiet all night, watching you and her." I point at Sabrina… "Eye fucking each other all night and I've had it up to here." I place my hand at the bottom of my chin. "All of yawl snooty ass's can go fuck yourself," I finish before I double over and vomit all over Hart's shoes.

"Trailer trash," Sabrina says to no one in particular.

"Enough, not another word out of you, Sabrina." His voice sounds adamant. "Damnit, Whitney," he grates out just before he lifts me into his arms and storms out the dining room and up the stairs to his bedroom.

"What are you doing?" I ask as Hart strips me and turns on the shower. He strips as well before urging me into the shower with him. The first spray of cold water hits my skin and I scream from its effects.

"I don't know what I'm going to do with you, Whitney Martin," Hart says as my teeth start to chatter and goosebumps appear on my skin. I feel like a fool so I remain quiet as the water wash over my flesh. *What have I done?* These are my last thoughts just before darkness claims me.

I awake the morning, to the pleasurable feeling of Hart French kissing my clit. I am powerless to resist as I place my hand on the back of his head and shove it further into my wetness.

"Mmmm," he growls against my hairless mound. "Your flavor has me addicted. You are so slippery and wet," his sexy voice makes me tremble as I grind against his mouth. My legs slide up and my thighs close to clutch about his head as his tongue darts in and out and swirls deliciously inside of my love tunnel. "Fuck," he roars and I can feel the terrible effort it takes for him to please me as he shows restraint. But my restraint is a goner as I cry out and squirt all of my love juices into his mouth. He laps away until he is filled and climbs up my body to settle between my thighs.

My inner muscles begin to quake as he covers my body and our eyes clash. His eyes continue to hold mine as he thrusts inside me to the hilt. I gasp aloud in splendorous pleasure as he begins to move inside my heat.

He withdraws his cock to the very tip and I cry out for more. He plunges back in, filling me up, as he starts to move inside me faster and faster. A pure sexual intent is driving my hips to meet him thrust for thrust. I cry out as his head bends down to take a hard nipple between his teeth and bite down. The electric shock is inexplicably sharp and pleasurable at the same time.

Hart takes that moment to swirl his hips at an angle and touch a spot within me that's never been touched before. My inside muscles contract around his hardness and I begin cumming and cumming and cumming like an unrelenting waterfall. My moans are lusty as I cry out over and over again.

Then he grips my hips as his shafts seems to grow even bigger. "I can't…I'm cumming," he groans and give up his hot seed to mix with my essence.

His hot seed spurts forth to heat up my insides most pleasurably. His spurts are a continuous flow as his cock is relentless, plunging into my core. I cry out again and join him with another explosion of my own.

Finally, my pulsating pussy releases him. He pulls me to his side and hugs me tightly. "Whitney, we need to have a serious talk, but first I need another nap." He closes his eyes and is knocked out.

Satiated and thoroughly loved, my eyes close and I join him in sleep. *He hasn't forgotten the debacle I made of myself last night. After all, it lingers in my immediate thoughts, even in my sleep.*

Chapter 19

HART

"I'm so sorry about last night, Hart. I don't know what got into me. Wait, that's a lie," she admits. "The way your parents received us and then the way your ex-girlfriend showed up messed me up."

"I love you, Whitney. You and no one else. I don't want you to ever doubt me. I'm a one-woman man, when I'm in love and I'm definitely in love with you."

"In my heart, I believe you. It's just that your parents…and Sabrina," she starts to say but I cut her off.

"I don't think my parents can comprehend how much our relationship means to me. They are confused by it, but they'll come around after seeing how much you really mean to me. They'll love you in time, like I do."

"Hart, I need to be honest with you. It hurts me terribly that your parents don't accept us. It just feels weird for us to be in a loving relationship or even to date for that matter in a house where I'm not welcome. I can't stay here any longer. I want to leave."

"Whitney, I already know that you're this amazing person and I'm so very deeply in love with you. I can only imagine the pain you feel about my parents and their way of thinking about our relationship, especially when I think about how wonderfully your mother accepted me. I can see why you're such a classy and beautiful woman. You have a wonderful example to follow. My grandfather was like that. He would've loved you from his first time setting eyes on you. He's who I've always tried to model myself after."

"I understand what you're saying, Hart. I really do. I wish I could've known your grandfather too, because if he was anything like you, he would've been easy for me to love. I wish your parents could see that true love just happens between two people for good reasons. Why can't they see that we care about each other and understand why we love each other? I don't see color when I look at you. I see you, my Hart of hearts, the man that I love."

"You are my everything, Whitney. I don't know if I can say anything to make a situation like this any better. I like to hope that things will get better for us with my family in time, and chances are they will, but who really knows? Still, whatever challenges we will face with my family, remember that you're not alone. There are lots of people out there in happy and wonderful relationships just like ours. We will make it through, with or without their blessings. You are mine and I am yours...I'm never, ever, letting you go."

The bedroom door creaks. Both Whitney and my head whip around to see my parents standing in the doorway looking repentant.

"Whitney wants to leave because of you two. If I have to choose between you and her, then by God, I'm choosing her," anger at their behavior blazes through me.

"We aren't making you choose, son. Your mother and I talked late into the night last night. We are ashamed of our disrespect of you, Whitney. You don't deserve the way we treated you. It seems we have some issues to work out that has nothing to do with you but everything to do with ourselves. For that, we are sorry." My dad discloses.

"Will you forgive us? Sabrina left early this morning…before sunrise. That was my doing and I'm really sorry for inviting her here. Please forgive me, both of you," my mother adds.

I look over at Whitney and she looks up at me. Her eyes are shimmering with tears that appear like precious diamonds. I pull her close to my side. "I'm telling you both now. The day will come when I'm going to make this woman my wife. She will have my children…your grandchildren. Can both of you accept that?"

There is a pause before they nod and speak. "Yes," they both reply in unison. I look into their eyes and see no deceit.

"What do you say, my love?" I wait to see what Whitney has to say. Because basically the fate of my parents are in her hands. No one has the right to hurt my Whitney. My parents included.

"I once heard a quote by an unknown. It went something like this: 'You can only heal if you forgive. You can only live in peace if you forgive. You can only let go if you forgive. Then and only then, can you truly heal and really love and be loved in return," she recites a quote and then says, "I forgive you both, because I love your son with my whole heart," she declares.

"I can see that your words are sincere and those are great words you just quoted, Whitney," my mother says with warmth in her voice

"I agree, young lady, you are wise beyond your years. I think we can learn a thing or two from you."

"I think we all can learn from each other. I love you, Whitney Martin."

"You know what?" she asks as we stare into each other eyes and our souls unite.

"What?" I ask as my parents look on with smiles on their faces.

"I love you more than I can say and I feel like the most blessed woman on earth to be loved by Hart…"

THE END

LOVING HART BY THERESA HODGE

Dearest Readers,

First, I want to thank God, for everything! I hope each one of you enjoyed reading Loving Hart. This is another of my special stories that I really enjoyed writing. To all my readers, I wish you great health, unsurmountable love and happiness. A special shout out goes to one of my wonderful readers, Dominique Whitney Morgan. I'm truly humbled by every one of my reader's support. Let love flow always.

Sincerely,

Theresa Hodge

P.S. Ladies, please don't forget to do self-breast checks. If you feel any abnormal lumps, please don't hesitate in seeing a doctor immediately and get yearly mammograms.

Check Out Other Titles By Theresa Hodge!